T0354569

Shamsuddin's
Grave

Shamsuddin's Grave

THE STORY OF A HOMELESS

PAROMITA GOSWAMI

PARTRIDGE
A Penguin Random House Company

To order additional copies of this book, contact
Partridge India
000 800 10062 62
orders.india@partridgepublishing.com

www.partridgepublishing.com/india

Dedication

To dearest Daddy and Ma. Love you always for watching over my back from heaven.

Acknowledgement

Thanks for choosing my work.

Your review is highly appreciated.

Before we proceed there are few people I would like to thank without whom my journey as an author would be incomplete.

First of all, Sri Sri Kanhailal (Lord Krishna, The saviour of the world)

My husband, Bhabotosh Mitra, whose encouraging words, pushed me to publish my work under all circumstances. You remain my first reader and my first critic ever. Thanks for being there always. Dhanak, for bearing with me when I could not give you the much needed attention. Your innocent encouraging words have never stopped ringing in my ears.

Krishanu Chatterjee, for the cover photograph that so perfectly matches the main character of my novel. My sisters

Panchatapa, Supriya, Sutapa who didn't mind answering my call, just about any time of the day, regarding my book. I appreciate your patience for listening to me whole heartedly always and then give your feedback. My relatives and friends of life whose encouraging words had always kept me going.

Mr. Rakesh Senger of Bachpan Bacaho Andolan,Delhi whose valuable inputs on Human Trafficking has helped me incredibly in my research work. Mr. Riyaz Ahmed and Shakuntala mam for their immense help in my research work.

Lastly to the team of Partridge India for sailing me through the whole course of publishing from ground zero.

Chapter One

Year 2003

"Hurr....rahh.... Hur.... raahh........."

The goat and its kids knew exactly what to do to that sound. It moved out of the barn and followed the man to the nearby field. The man left it there for grazing and came back to the house. He sat down on the varendah by the kitchen door wiping his face with his *gamcha*.

"Mami!" he called out to the lady inside the kitchen.

A lean old lady came out with a cup of tea and two biscuits in her hand. She handed them both to Shamsuddin.

"Aren't you late for work?" the lady asked.

He shook his head and took a sip of tea from the cup. He replied munching the biscuit, "I have to look for new job."

It was not a new conversation for both of them. It was more or less like exchanging greetings every morning. Each knew the question and the following answer. Actually their morning had never been any different for the past couple of years, the same morning routine of taking the goats to the field and the same red tea and biscuits. Only the house looked gloomier over those years which once had been the epitome of all events in the neighborhood.

"Why don't you go to my brother's place? He has shifted here recently. Surely he might need help," the lady suggested.

"You think so? Alright I shall visit him then," saying he got up. He washed his cup from the well in the courtyard and put it beside the kitchen door.

The lady picked up the cup and gently placed it in a corner away from all the other utensils in her kitchen. She was not the only one doing it. Coming from a well known Brahmin family allowing a Muslim inside the house premises let alone share utensils was totally against the rituals practiced by the Hindus in this part of the country. The nation may be celebrating golden jubilee of Independent India but it has failed to wipe the scars of partitions from both the communities till date. And Guwahati, the gateway of Northeast India, was no different. For ages the city has been a dumb witness to the tension prevailing between different communities which burst out on minimum provocation be it Hindu-Muslim or Bengali-Assamese or Hindi -Assamese or the tribal and non-tribal tribes. And adding flame to the fire are the political system and insurgent groups that keep no stone unturned for their own interest. In all these modus operandi it is the common man who bears the bruise. Kalapahar, the resettlement colony of the Hindu Bengali refugees from Bangladesh, in the outskirts of Guwahati city was no different.

The handful of migrated Hindu families who first came down to settle here after losing everything in partition had had a hard time surviving. Snehlata was one of them. Her husband would be out for work most of the time and she had the responsibility to up bring her children single handedly where surviving itself was a big question. The area at that time was a marshy land with no civic amenities whatsoever. Earthquakes, flood, infiltration of wild animals from the nearby forest, criminal activities were part of the daily life of the residents in this area. And to top that the inhabitants were poverty stricken. People somehow managed their lives by helping each other in need and thus the society developed. And today, it was one of the most sought after developing neighborhood in close proximity to the Guwahati city. The place had everything now from supermarkets, offices, schools, hotels and restaurant and with it came the employment opportunities for many.

From having nothing after partition to earning a respectable lifestyle the people here had done it all. And Snehlata was no exception. She was merely ten years old when she had lost her mother and stepped into her mother's shoes for raising her young siblings. Her father was a traveler and left the children under the care of servants back at home in Shillong. She left her studies too young to take up the household work which she had mastered with perfection over the years. Her illiteracy was never a hindrance in her life. She was a mute learner and love to read from her brother's books. The beautiful girl had slowly turned into a shy and introvert young lady. She was a good listener but not a good speaker. She could never stand up for her own rights. Not even when her father remarried a girl almost her age and married her off at a mere thirteen years of age to a man twice her age. That was the time of partition and tension prevailed in the state of Assam as well. The uncertainty in people's lives clearly shown on all face be it Hindu or Muslim. The Bengali Hindu families, who decided to migrate to India, were proverty striken. Both her father and husband had lost all their properties in East Pakistan. Starting from zero with her husband had been very difficult for her. And she never forgot the pain of rendering homeless and needy. Thus she helped everybody irrespective of their caste, religion and creed in her own way. Her home in Kalapahar had sheltered many, who like her had nowhere to go and this had earned her both accolade and disgrace. But she chose to stick to her deeds. And thus for the last ten years Shamsuddin had a place to call home.

Chapter Two

"*Mama*!" Shamsuddin called out from the gate.

Latika opened the gate and saw Shamsuddin for the first time. He wore a lungee double tied above his knees with a neatly buttoned worn-out shirt and a red *gamcha* around his waist like a belt. His large expressive eyes and unruly hair complemented his skin tone that matched the color of the rusted gate.

"How are you *Didi*? Is M*ama* at home?" He smiled.

"Yes. Come inside," Latika replied.

"*Na hoibo*. Please tell him it's Shamsuddin," he said still standing by the gate.

Latika went inside wandering about the man and sent her father outside. The old man pulled up a chair across in the courtyard and sat down. Then looked at the man at the gate and said, "*Ke re Shamsuddin! Bhetore aye.*"

"*Na, Mami* has asked me to meet you. Is there any work?" he said stepping inside the premises.

"Yes there is. Can you help us unpack and arrange the house?"

"*Ho,*" saying he squatted on the ground with a smiling face.

"Well then, Latika will tell you what all needs to be done." The old man called for Latika and went inside.

By the time Latika came out Shamsuddin had taken off his shirt and stood in his vest with his *gamcha* tied across his forehead. He was all set to start the work. Latika gave him instructions and he worked to perfection shifting furniture and boxes from one room to another.

It was much easier for him than loading and unloading bags of cement which he was doing for the last couple of months. Lately his back problem was taking the toll and hence he was looking for an alternative job. However, today was a breezy change for him than his usual work and he wasn't tired at all. He worked till lunch and usually had his meal from the roadside shops. But it came as a big surprise for him when Latika offered him lunch.

After freshening up he sat in the courtyard. He had never been offered meal in any Hindu household he had worked before. Eventually Latika's little gesture set him thinking as he waited for his meal. He was even more surprised when she called him inside the house to have his lunch. He was reluctant as he knew the rituals Hindu households followed against the Muslims or rather the Miya Muslims of Bengali origin. They hardly allowed these Muslims in the house let alone offer meal. He hesistantly came by the entrance door and waited.

"Why are you standing there?" said Latika, "please come inside."

"It's fine," he replied with a smile still standing at the door.

"No. You may come inside and sit here," said Latika pulling a table and a chair in the hall.

Shamsuddin took off his chappal and walked in. He sat down on the chair with a vague expression on his face. He knew very well that Latika was brought up in Delhi and was totally ignorant of the customs practiced here. He saw the maid, a Hindu lady, piercing him with her eyes in total disbelief from the kitchen. He lowered his lashes and sat tight. Latika served him lunch. It was a plate full of rice, dal and fish curry. The food made him forget everything else. It was ages since he had had a home cooked meal. He pounced on it hungrily. Latika kept reloading his plate till he could eat no more. His eyes smeared with tears as he finished off the last bit of rice in the plate and gulped down the glass of water. After finishing his lunch he carefully took away his plate and washed it outside. Then came back and cleaned the table with his *gamcha*. It was the only way he could rectify the blunder that was done on his behalf.

Latika had seen this practice many times in her house. But she had always defied it. Her mother had been a firm believer of rituals throughout her life and she had valid reasons for it. Migrating from Bangladesh was not easy for her family. The wounds had always remained fresh in her heart. But Latika was different. She was the woman of the new millineum. Her father's transferable job landed her in boarding school at a very young age where her interaction with students of different communites unbiased her mindset in her growing years. Later after completing MBA she shifted to Delhi and started her career in a reputed organization. She was the independent woman of today's generation who always believed in making a change other than taking a hefty pay cheque at the end of the month. She also worked as a volunteer with an NGO that worked for the urban slum development. However, coming back to Guwahati after so many years was a decision she had to take the harder way. Life had not been easy for her lately and after her mother's demise there was no looking back. She came back with her ailing father leaving everything behind to make a fresh start in Guwahati and this time she had made up her mind to devote herself completely to social service. She had joined an NGO that worked for the urban development in Guwahati. But her interaction with Shamsuddin alerted her of the upcoming challenges in her work.

Shamsuddin however, had a high thinking for her. Such generosity in a Hindu home was totally unexpected by him. The simple meal had bonded him to Latika forever. Though he had been staying in a Hindu home for the last ten years but he could never even think of crossing his limits. All these years he made a practice of leaving the house early in the morning after tea and returned only after dinner so that people hardly took any notice of him. Yet the community never stopped accusing Snehlata for allowing a Muslim to stay at her house premises. He was totally amazed by the simple gesture Latika showed to him which he had almost forgotten over the years. Life had been very difficult for him since his childhood.

Chapter Three

Even after five decades of India's partition the plight of Shamsuddin's family had not changed. He was born in a small village in Barpeta district of Assam. His father was a poor farmer who owned a bit of farming land near the bank of Beki River, a tributary of Brahmaputra. But the yearly floods in Brahmaputra River eroded the farming land well enough to deprive the family a healthy means of income. Most of year he and his children worked in other's faming land or fisheries to feed the family.

Shamsuddin was no special. He was the youngest of the six sons and three daughters in the family and by the age of six he too started earning for the family. Sometimes herding cattle, sometimes as a laborer or whatever opportunity came his way. But money was never enough for the family.

Eventually the children grew up and married and took to their own ways.

Shamsuddin was left behind with his widowed mother and his wife. He was the man of the family now. There was not much left for him in their farming land after his father's demise as the brothers had divided it among themselves and sold their share to the landlord of the village. The landlord even pressurized Shamsuddin to sell his portion but he denied.

He took pride and worked in his field but no matter how hard he worked flood would always destroy his hard labor. He was bound to take up other work or borrow money from the landlord who in turn would take something or the other as security from him. He knew that he would not be able to keep his land and house off the hands of the landlord for very long and had to think for some other way out.

He learnt that government was compensating those affected by floods but it never reached their family. Against his will he went to the government offices to seek his compensation. He was quite surprised to know that his family did not even exist in government papers. He had heard about illegal migrants and his family was branded as one. It was not his fault if his father chose to live in India after partition and he had never acquired any formal papers from his father. They were too illiterate to know about India's partition and then later the birth of Bangladesh.

His father and his father's father had always been busy meeting the needs of the family rather than think of the international borders and current affairs. But Shamsuddin now knew that like many villagers he too had been branded as an illegal migrant from Bangladesh in the government statistics.

By the age of twenty five he already fathered five children but his family's condition had not changed even a bit. What he disliked most was he was following his father's path. Instead of sending the children to school he was doing the same as his father had done with him, earning to meet the ends of the family. But then he could not find a way out. Although he wanted to change their condition for the better, send them to schools, educate them give them a better life. But didn't know how?

Then his Allah listened to him. During 1990, President's Rule was imposed in Assam. With the announcement of fresh elections several political parties visited their village and promised to listen to their plight giving them a ray of hope. During this time few young men from the village joined these parties in campaign rallies and in return earned a handsome amount. Shamsuddin was one of them. He would go to rallies in the nearby village with these parties and in return would get some money. It was a decent change from what he had been doing. And it also helped him to know the world beyond his village. This brought in a major change in him. He started thinking big and knew deep down that he had to get out of his village if he wanted a decent life.

He came to Guwahati with big dreams in the first chance. It was difficult to leave his family behind but they understood. First few months in the big city were very good for him as election was due and the party needed people like him. Few months later when he returned home he had made good money. His family was very pleased with him. He told his family about the big opportunities of making money in big city, the lifestyle of people, the big market, motors cars and above all to get compensation for his land from the government. So when he told about his decision to go back to Guwahati to make money his family did not hesitate.

However by then scene in Guwahati had changed, election was over and party rallies were no more conducted. When Shamsuddin returned to Guwahati he was no longer needed by the party. So he was left to fend for himself in the big city. Days passed without proper food and shelter. And the thought of surviving in the big city was a big question for him. But the thought that his family banked on him kept him going. Finally one day he met Jamal, one of his friends from the village who worked as a mason.

Jamal owned a small rented room in the slums near Kalapahar area. Jamal not only let him stay in his place but also let him work with him. Shamsuddin could never ask for more. He worked with Jamal as a construction worker to build new houses or renovating old houses. During one such contract Shamsuddin came in contact with Snehlata. She had a renovation job which was taken up by Jamal's contractor. It lasted for few months. Both Jamal and Shamsuddin were assigned the job at her house by their contactor.

Shamsuddin was very touched by Snehlata's kindness which none had showed him so far in Guwahati. In return he started doing petty household jobs for her like getting veggies from the market or calling a rickshaw or booking her gas cylinder. In return Snehlata gave him little money. He kept visiting her now and then even when the renovation job was over. And when he told her he was going home for Eid she gave him money to purchase something for his family. After many years he and his family had a nice time during Eid. He believed he had made the right decision to go to Guwahati and so did his family.

But things did not remain the same. When he returned after Eid once again he had to face hardship. Jamal was down with jaundice and could not continue to work in Guwahati anymore. Eventually he had to give up his rented room as he could not afford to pay the rents without work. Shamsuddin was in no position to rent a room on his own. Even while staying with Jamal he did not make contribution as in terms of money but did the dishes, cooking and cleaning.

Once again he had no place to stay. His work also could not help him much. It was a difficult time for Shamsuddin. Monsoon was on its way which meant for some months there will be no construction work and Shamsuddin had to look for an alternate work too.

Sitting on the pavement he smoked his *biri* thinking of the hard days ahead. He was back to square one once more. There were several people who shared the pavement with him, people who were homeless. He befriended some of them. But the company he chose this time was bad. These were daily laborers who worked very hard the whole day and in the evening ended up in local brothels.

Shamsuddin met Geeta during one such visit. She worked as a maid in the daytime and in the evening as a local hooker. Her family disowned her when her husband eloped with other woman. Surviving as a lone woman was very difficult for her and life had taught her the hard way. Geeta lived on her own terms. She earned well as a maid and also owned a small room in the slum area. She had thought of settling down many times but her wounds of life were fresh enough to let any man in. Hence she did not hook to any single partner. As when need be she would throw them out of her life.

When Shamsuddin met her he was desperately looking for a shelter at night. Geeta liked his simplicity instantly and allowed him to stay in her room but on her terms. He did everything she asked for except money. She abused him and even tortured him physically. In a way all her grudges against her husband and her life was targeted on Shamsuddin but Shamsuddin would not break. He knew he had no alternative and she was her only source of hope if he wanted to survive in Guwahati. So he never gave up on her atrocities.

Chapter Four

Monsoons poured in within few weeks causing flood situation in the entire state. Guwahati city was also not spared. The rain water had seeped into houses and buildings making it impossible for people to reside anymore. People took refuge in the schools and colleges that are transformed into temporary relief shelters. Flood that year had hit a new record in the state before the water finally receded leaving behind a trail of huge damage to the lives and property. The train and road transportation were disrupted in many parts of the state.

The slum area of Kalapahar located adjacent to the Bharulu River, a tributary of Brahmapura, also bore a devastating look. People were forced to live in relief camps. However many houses that were located a little uphill remained unaffected by the flood. Geeta's house was one of them. Staying in Geeta's house Shamsuddin considered himself lucky enough to survive but the thought of his family back home made him anxious.

He knew very well that during monsoons his village gets affected by the flood but this time he had more reasons to worry. Firstly, he was not around to help his family and secondly, the radio news updated him about the plight of villages in Barpeta. Flood in Brahmaputra had washed away many villages in that district. He didn't even know whether his family survived or not. He was anxious to reach his family but was unable as the routes were still disrupted. He prayed to Allah for their safety day and night. That was the time when Geeta shared his pain. The pain of separation from her husband and his fear of loss for his family brought them together.

It was almost a fortnight before the bus and train services resumed. Shamsuddin caught the first train back to his village. However, by then all the hell had broken loose at his village. His home and land were submerged in the flood water. Luckily his family had survived. He found them in one relief camps. His mother had died and his youngest son was missing. But he was relieved to find the survivors of his family. He took his family to his distant cousin's place in another village which was unaffected by flood.

His cousin was financially well off and had an ailing wife with no children. He was very pleased and relived to see Shamsuddin's family safe and made all arrangements to rehabilitate them at his house. Shamsuddin could never ask for more. Together they tried to look for the missing child but all the efforts went in vain. Slowly the family tried to come out of the immediate loss. Even with all the generosity shown by his cousin Shamsuddin knew he had to earn enough money to raise his family independently. For now they can stay at his cousin's place but sooner he had to arrange accommodation for them. Shamsuddin stayed with them for few weeks and returned back to Guwahati. He had only one thing in mind to earn more money.

Back in Guwahati Geeta gave him a warm welcome that he had never imagined in his dreams. It was more than home coming for him. She cooked for him and served him hot meals. She also did all the cleaning herself and even made his bed. She even asked him about his family and empathized with him. Overall she behaved as a totally different person which Shamsuddin was not familiar with all these months. However, it pleased him considerably that there was someone in this city who cared for him so much. Geeta's changed attitude had brought Shamsuddin close to her. At least there was this person who gave him comfort when he returned from work totally exhausted in the evening.

Geeta too started enjoying his company as a man in her life. Years of separation from her husband and mistreated by men folk in the society she kind of became rebellious. She picked up men on her own and kicked them out once the need was over. But with Shamsuddin her parameters had been different from the beginning. He had stood by her even after experiencing the worst of her wherein others fled. And when she saw him weeping for his wife and family she knew that this man really cared for his family no matter what.

She always wanted a man like him in her life who could love her so much and care for her. And it somehow fanned her buried emotions for a man. So when Shamsuddin returned he saw a different Geeta, one who was a submissive woman. And this time Shamsuddin could not stop himself from reciprocating her. Earlier it was his materialistic and physical need that prompted him to stay at Geeta's place day after day facing the bruise of insult and agony but this time he opted to stay for love and emotions.

Months of separation from his wife and children created a craving for them in Shamsuddin but he knew too well that this separation was earning them food and clothes. So he knew he cannot leave Guwahti to return to them until he had saved good money. In Geeta he saw a vent to take out his emotions that he had settled within him all these months out of sepeartion from his family. He had started liking her and together they had created their own love nest. Each knew the limitations they were bound in yet nothing stopped them from coming closer to each other. In a way they were complimenting each other's loss. He knew it was wrong as he stayed in the house like man and wife while back home his wife was counting days of his return. But then it was difficult to resist the temptation of being loved.

Each night when Geeta came to him and showered her love over him all he could remember is make love to her. At that moment only thoughts of Geeta mattered to him. Her caresses, her kisses, her moans, her need would fire up his body till he could take no longer and take her all within him till each lay panting beside the other blissfully happy and satisfied. What happens next is what Shamsuddin could not take any further.

Each time after his physical intimacy with Geeta his wife's face would loom up in front of his eyes and a sense of guilt overpowered him. It was not because of sex but because of depriving his wife off her rights. At that moment all the happiness and satisfaction that he had experienced a few minutes ago turned futile and was replaced by his selfishness. He had been selfish to see his interest only and not bother about his wife's pain. He wished his wife was with him instead. Geeta would sometimes console him saying that he was a man and there was nothing wrong in fulfilling his needs. It was good to hear such words as they encouraged him and he would be ready to take another plunge on Geeta before the night ended.

Chapter Five

Shamsuddin knew he cannot betray his wife for long. He still needed courage to meet her eyes and face his children. Although he knew with the long distance between them his wife would never know about his affair and he can continue his relation with Geeta. However, the husband and father within him would not give away so easily. He had to earn enough money to go back to his family.

He worked very hard. Whatever opportunity came his way he would grab it to make money. Pulling rickshaw, as a daily waged laborer or as a vegetable vender he was doing everything to make money to go back to his wife. He worked hard the whole day and at night allowed Geeta to screw him. Sometimes he liked sometimes he resisted but not for long. Although he shared everything with Geeta but she knew there was something amiss in the relationship. It was not turning up as it was nurtured to be. Over the months it was turning into a physical intimacy only. Emotionally she sensed a change in Shamsuddin's attitude. No matter what she did Shamsuddin remained with her physically only. Mentally he still belonged to his wife. And at last Geeta lost the battle. She knew she could not keep this simple man for long and once again became her old self. She threw Shamsuddin out of her life and moved on.

It was a relief for Shamsuddin to come out of the guilt. Sitting on the pavement again near the road he lighted his *biri* and puffed circles of smoke in the air. All his stress was released. He took train to his village the next day. It had been almost a year since he visited his family last. He had made good money this time and bought a beautiful sari for his wife. His children too must have grown up now. He was sure his cousin was taking good care of his family. He had made a game plan for them. He would marry off his eldest daughter this year and shift his family to a new house in the village. And in his new home he would show his wife how much he loved her. He took the train and went to meet his family in the village.

His dreams shattered the moment he met Amina, his wife, at his cousin's place. She was eight months pregnant. It did not take Shamsuddin to make the calculations which failed against him. He was separated from her more than a year now and she was carrying a child in her womb. For few minutes Shamsuddin was in shock. He didn't want to believe what he saw.

While going back to Guwahti, leaving his family behind, Shamsuddin had completely forgotten about his all time sick sister-in-law. Obviously that was not an appropriate time to think of her. At that time all he needed was a shelter for his family and his cousin had offered help without a question. What more could he ask for? It was the best possible solution he could think of for his family at that time. It never occurred to him that Amina would not be safe at his cousin's place.

The moment Shamsuddin was gone, Farruk, his cousin could not resist putting his hands off Amina. His sick wife had never really been competent enough to take care of him as a husband. She was more occupied with her health problems than his needs. Although his physical needs were well taken care of by village brothels however, Amina's presence in the house highly flamed his need for an heir. A mother of four, Amina displayed all the qualities of a complete woman and he repected her even more when she refused to his advances. He found a dedicated wife in her saving herself for a man who lived miles away with no certainty of coming back soon.

For months Amina resisted all the advances Farruk made towards her but there was no slightest decline from his side. Each time he would come up with something new to woo her. Amina knew very well that till her husband returned she had to bear with this man yet she held herself up by all means. Nevertheless Farruk's persuasion time and again did slightly mould her inside. She could see how well he was taking care of her children in spite of her refusal. Her sons were now going to school and Farruk was also looking for a suitable match for her elder daughter. As a man he was fulfilling all the duties which Shamshuddin should have done as a father. But he had never been around to even look after their well being. Moreover, financially too Farruk was much well off than Shamsuddin. Then one day she heard rumors of Shamsuddin's affair with a Hindu woman. One of Jamal's friends saw the two together and spread the word back in the village. The news somehow reached Amina's ears. She couldnot believe it initially but when for months there was still no trace of Shamshuddin's return his betrayal ignited hatred in her. She could never think of forgiving him in her lifetime. Her hatred for Shamsuddin lessened the gap between herself and Farruk. Meanwhile the untimely demise of her sick sister-in-law persuaded Amina to take the last plunge and she readily accepted Farruk's proposal.

Farruk had promised to take care of her and her children forever provided she quits Shamsuddin. Amina never looked back and Farruk kept his words. Shortly he married off Amina's elder daughter too and took good care of her children's education and upbringing. The children already had high regards for Farruk. There was nothing more Amina could ask for and she gave herself in to him.

Standing by the gate Shymashuddin finally realize that he had lost Amina forever. The look in her eyes said it all and the bulge of her womb the evidence of her betrayal. Hatred and anger gripped him within and he came charging towards her. He was almost ready to strike his fist on her face when Farruk came in between them.

"Dare you touch her again I shall break your arms," said Farruk firmly and shoved him off the way.

"You have no right to talk in between," shouted Shamsuddin. "Get out of my way or else I ...." Amina cut short his words.

31

"Why did you come back now?" she demanded. "You have lost your space in our lives. We don't want to see you again. Go away!" she cried.

Shamsuddin could not believe what he just heard. His Amina was asking him to go away. "Amina I am your husband! What are you saying?" he pleaded.

"Now you remember that? Where were you when we needed you? Making money and enjoying. Did it ever occur to you how much we needed you here?" she cried.

"There is no point in standing here. She has made her choice, Shamsuddin," said Farruk. "Two years is a really long time. You have nothing left here. So go away! "

Shamsuddin looked at Amina standing behind. She stood with her chin up yet her eyes were moist and lips tight. He got his answer. She indeed had made the choice but he wanted to hear from her.

"Amina! You couldn't mean it?" he asked in a trembling voice.

She did not answer him but turned back and walked away.

Shamsuddin could not take it anymore. His ego was badly bruised and he wanted to teach her a lesson. He yelled and ran after her.

"You will not live anymore." He grabbed her neck and pulled her out of the house. Amina shrieked and Farruk hurled at him to rescue her. The men fought till Shamsuddin was thrown out of the house and the door shut on his face.

In one stroke his life went upside down. His wife had abandoned him. He wept bitterly sitting on the road outside the house but none of the villagers came to help though most of them had gathered around the house to watch the show. He was hurt more by his male ego then Amina's adultery. Before leaving he gave a last shot towards the door that still was shut but nobody responded. He moved on.

Later while having tea at the village shop he learnt that the villagers thought of Farruk as a very good man who had the guts to take the responsibility of a distressed woman whose husband had abandoned her for a Hindu woman. After his wife's demise Farruk had married her. Shamsuddin wondered if his son's still wanted him.

He retraced his path back to the house. He was sure his eldest son would understand and forgive him but it did not happen. In fact his son held him responsible for all the miseries they had to face in life. He held his father responsible for the loss of their home and grandmother. Shamsuddin was hearbroken when his son said Farruk was their *Abba* now.

Chapter Six

He didn't remember how he boarded the train back to Guwahati. He sat on the pavement outside the railway station and cried bitterly. He had no one to turn to in his life. His family had abandoned him, he had no home. He could not go back to Geeta either as she had shut him out of her life. He felt very lonely.

He thought of going back to his village and start all over again but the thought terrorized him. There was no house, no land and no family back in his village. And maybe the people there too didn't want him anymore. He wept inconsolably.

He walked towards the Brahmaputra River that flowed in the vicinity. For days he just walked near the banks of Brahmaputra in search of solace. He kept on walking from one place to another tired, hungry and sleepy. Yet he did not stop to rest. Like an insane he wandered on the banks. Many times the urge to commit suicide crossed his mind but something within him stopped him. All his energy and thoughts were focused on his wife and children. He could not believe that they had disowned him. Throughout his life he had only been thinking for their betterment. Even while spending penniless days on the pavement and sleeping empty stomach the only thought gave him peace that at least his children were not sleeping without food. Though he had not been able to do much for them but he always wanted them to have the best. As a father he did what he could do his best and as far as Amina was concerned he knew he had committed a sin. But should she be so harsh to punish him this way? The thought troubled him so much that he was on the verge of losing his sanity.

One evening while sitting on the bank of the river he heard the Azan. He followed the sound and reached a dargah. He saw people offering their prayer. He sat down on the steps of the entrance. He felt very weak and suddenly he blacked out. When he opened his eyes he saw an old man sitting beside him. The white beard and the matching white attire glistened in the light of the room. The old man looked like an angel. Shamsuddin tried to sit up but the old man stopped him.

"You are too weak to get up my child. You must eat something first," said the old man. He offered a glass of juice to Shamsuddin.

Shamsuddin gulped down the entire juice in one go. The glass was refilled. This time he took some time to gulp down the juice. The old man gestured him to take rest.

Shamsuddin slept peacefully for next few hours. Later the old man brought him dinner which he finished hungrily and once again went back to sleep. He slept for the next whole day and finally woke up in the afternoon. His body had regained some of the lost strength. He got up and bathed. Then after lunch came to meet the old man who was addressing some devotees visiting the dargah.

"Whatever Allah has assigned for you will always come back to you. Nobody can seize it from you. So have faith in his actions and serve him selflessly….. "

The wordings kept ringing in Shamsuddin's ears. It filled him with a new hope inside, a hope of reuniting with his family one day. It gave him a new strength to come up from the broken phase and he recovered steadily to bounce back once more. He stayed in the dargah for some days. And each day very sincerely he heard the old man addressing the visitors. The teachings strengthened him and showed him a different perspective of life that of forgiveness and hope. Each day his faith on Allah grew and he believed one day everything will be alright. And he should be prepared for that day.

With the new strength and hope he took leave of the old man and started afresh. He reached Kalapahar and looked for job. He was young and a well built man. So getting job was not difficult for him. Once again he started working as a daily laborer. In the day time he worked his soul off and at night slept on the pavement. This time he made sure he avoided the bad company. Sometimes lying on the pavement at night he analyzed his life. He tried to decipher the events that caused his family to disown him. The more he analyzed it concluded for a house of his own. He came to the conclusion that all these miseries he faced today was only because of this only reason. If he had had one then he would have brought his family here and the misery would have been averted. He blamed himself for not looking into this angle earlier.

The mere thought of owning a house and bringing his family over relieved him of all the stress that he had been troubling him since. It was a magical thought that gave him strength and a motive to struggle all the odds in Guwahati. The thought was so strong that it made him believe that his wife and children had actually not betrayed him at all. In his dream he would see his house where his wife was cooking for him and his children clinging on to him adoringly. He started living his dream. And it gave him immense strength to fight the loneliness that engulfed him. All his earnings would be directed towards owning his small house where he would live happily with his family everafter. And thus his days passed with new enthusiasm.

He discussed the finance required to make a house and calculated his savings. He felt a new kick within and was excited. Every day he would sit and count his saving. It was a new excitement for him to see how much more he had to save the next day to achieve a particular target. One day when he was counting his money he saw one of his pavement buddies eyeing him. He knew instantly that his money was not safe with him anymore. Although the amount was not very huge yet he had to look for some other alternative to keep his money safe. Next day he went to the bank to open a saving amount. They asked him for his residence proof and photo identity which he failed to produce. He could not open an account in the bank. He tried several other banks in the vicinity but everywhere he was asked to produce these legal documents.

He did not know what to do about it. So far he had never thought of these documents. All his life he had been too busy to earn bread and butter for his family that an important document like ration card or photo identity was out of question for him. He also remembered that back in his village when he had gone to government offices for filing compensation for his land he found that his family did not existed on government papers and he was branded an illegal migrant. At that time too he had ran from pillar and post but could not find any help. And this time he had no clue how to figure it out. His illiteracy and poverty was the major hindrance in his path. He sincerely needed someone to help him out.

He could only think of Snehlata at that time of need. So one day he reached Snehlata's doorstep. He knew she was the only person whom he could confide to. He told her openly about the dream of owning a house in Guwahati and how much he only trusted her for it. She listened to him and offered to help him though she knew getting legal documents for opening bank account was not possible. Instead she offered him to keep his savings safe with her. It seemed the easiest possible way and he trusted her for it. So next day he brought her all his savings and asked her to keep it safe. And thus his daily visit to her house started. He would come to her after his day's work and deposit the money in her hands. And she would offer him tea and ask him to fetch her goats from the field or get veggies from the market.

Days passed and Shamsuddin was more of a part of her household now. He would help her in her petty jobs like mending the barn or fencing the courtyard or watering the kitchen garden. There was a bond of faith in them. She would ask for his health if he did not turn out someday while he would take her to the temple if nobody was there to escort her. When the winter set in sleeping on the pavement was difficult and she eventually allowed him to stay at her house when he had no option. However, she allowed him to sleep in the barn to avoid the neighbor's confrontation. Shamsuddin could not ask for more and did not mind sharing it with the goats. And thus Shamsuddin passed his days at Snehlata's house with a dream which both shared. He never went back to his village after that day however each night he dreamt of his family in his dream house.

Chapter Seven

Snehlata was happy to have him in her house. Her children were grown up and settled in different parts of the country. Her husband's work kept him busy and he usually returned late at night. So having Shamsuddin in the house premises was more of a help to her. Apart from helping her in petty works his presence at night also helped as security of the house. It was an old fashioned house with a big courtyard in the middle. The living quarters and the kitchen area were separated by the courtyard. The barn was at the other end of the house adjoining the kitchen area.

Usually when Shamsuddin returned from work Snehlata would be in the kitchen cooking dinner. After freshening up he would sit on the verandah outside the kitchen and discussed his day's activity with her before handing her the saved money. Snehlata would calculate the money in

Shamsuddin's presence and write the amount in a small notebook that she always kept in the kitchen shelf. That way they both knew the total amount deposited with her. Shamsuddin would wait till her dinner preparation. Then when she went inside the living room to watch television he would retire to the barn. This was the routine they followed for months.

****

That day, after working in Latika's house, Shamsuddin returned home early. He did not stop for freshening up himself instead sat on the verandah waiting for Snehlata to give him attention.

"What happened to you? You are early today." Snehlata inquired from inside the kitchen.

He did not answer rather smiled back at her.

"Did you go to my brother's place today?" asked Snehlata from the kitchen door.

Shamsuddin looked up ginning at her from ear to ear. He was looking like a boy who found a new toy.

"*Ho*! I went. And also had lunch there," he replied excitedly. "You know *Mami*, she asked me indoors and made me sit at the table. And you know what! She served me food with her own hands. Can you believe that?"

Snehlata quite easily understood his excitement. She smiled at him and said, "Latika has always been like that. That's very sweet of her." She completed her chore and came out in the verandah. "What did she serve you at lunch?"

"She served me fish curry till I was full," he replied. "She is very good. Isn't she *Mami*?"

Snehlata pulled up a stool and sat down. "I wish we all thought the same way Shamsuddin. But people here won't change and we have to accept it that way. Latika has spent most of her life mostly outside Guwahati. Staying in big city, you know, she has developed a different mindset. Had my sister-in-law been alive it would have been a different scenario altogether today."

"*Ho Mami*. You are correct. But I am really very happy today. Thank you for sending me there," said Shamsuddin. "I am a poor man and that too Miya Muslim. Nobody even think of us as a human being let alone serve food. You are different *Mami* and so is your niece. You two are angels sent by Allah to help people like us," he murmured hiding his moist eyes.

Snehlata sighed and said, "Things are changing Shamsuddin. Today's generation do not think like us. They have more exposure than us and have a better thinking. Our generation had bore the bruise of hatred and that too not once but twice. So our generation thinks like that but I am glad that the future is bright for all of us."

Shamsuddin took out some notes wrapped in his lungee and handed them to her saying, "I have to go there tomorrow too. Here is the money for today."

Snehlata counted the money and reached for her notebook from the shelf. She wrote the amount in front of him and added the total balance. Then said, "Its five thousand nine hundred and eighty five rupees now, Shamsuddin. Tomorrow it will be six thousand plus."

"*Ho Mami*."

Their conversation ended and both went back to their work, Snehlata to cook dinner and Shamsuddin to freshen up before retiring for the day.

Next morning he went to Latika's house again after having his red tea and biscuit. Latika had already started the work by the time he reached. She was all set to color her room. Dressed in a worn out jeans and Tee with a bandana on her head she was mixing the paint when Shamsuddin arrived. She signed him to pick up a worn out shirt from the chair and join her in painting the room.

They started the work. By lunch most of the work was complete to Latika's expectation. She called off the work when her maid informed that the lunch was ready. Once again Shamsuddin was offered lunch and this time the maid served him. Both finished their lunch and went back to work. By evening the entire room was painted. Sunshine yellow donned the walls while the ceiling was painted white. It was finally to her satisfaction before she called off for the day. She paid Shamsuddin his due amount and asked him to come again the next day.

Following morning Shamsuddin came as usual but Latika was not in the house. He completed his work as the maid instructed him to do. Latika had detailed her about the work that needed to be done. He was served lunch again as usual in the house and by evening he had finished all the work. Shamsuddin now waited for his payment. The maid informed him that Latika had been out to the city and might be late. He decided to wait for her outside.

A little after dusk Latika returned home. She saw Shamsuddin waiting for her outside.

"Shamsuddin you are still here? What happened?" she inquired.

"*Didi* I have finished the work," he replied.

"Oh! Let me see." She went inside and asked him to come along. After a brief scrutiny she handed him the payment and asked him to sit down. Shamsuddin sat down on a stool in the hall.

She went inside the kitchen and prepared tea. She poured it in two cups and handed one cup to Shamsuddin. She sat down on a chair across the table sipping her tea looking at Shamsuddin. Shamsuddin felt her gaze on him but he kept his eyes on the floor and silently sipped his tea.

"Where do you stay Shamsuddin?" Latika asked suddenly.

"Why? Don't you know Didi?"

Latika shook her head.

"I stay at *Mami*'s house," he answered.

"Oh! That's good. So how long you have been there?" She was interested to know.

"Too long! Maybe ten years or so. I forgot the count," he replied.

"And your family?"

The question set his heart racing. "In the village," he replied after a pause. Earlier he avoided answering that question but then realized no answer raised suspicion and he didn't want that.

"Ok. I was thinking if you could take me to the slum area tomorrow," she asked.

Shamsuddin was surprised to hear that. He nodded and asked, "I shall but *Didi*, why would you go there?"

Latika smiled and replied, "It's my work area. See you tomorrow at 6.00 am then. Fine?"

"*Ho.*" He got up quietly and as usual washed his cup outside before placing it carefully on the table in the hall.

Latika was quite excited about her new job. The entire day she had spent in the Head Office in the city and was assigned work at their nodal office in Kalapahar area. She was to report her joining the next day and was quite excited about the new place. Although she had the experience of working in the urban slum in Delhi yet she knew it would be entirely different experience in Kalapahar. She thought Shamsuddin being a local could give her a better input about the slum community and hence decided to visit the area with Shamsuddin the next morning first before reporting to her office.

Chapter Eight

Early next morning Latika set out with Shamsuddin to visit the slum community. It was situated in the vicinity of the Bharalu River on the other side of the neighborhood. The river served as a natural drainage system of the city carrying the waste of the colonies to the River Brahmaputra.

She parked her car off the road and walked the dirt lane along the Bharalu River. As far as she could see the entire embankment were encroached with make shift houses and shops. A small temple was also visible at a distance. These structures were built on bamboo stilt with a fencing made of bamboo lattice that served as walls with only one outlet in the front with thatched roofs or tin sheets. With so much encroachment the river was reduced to a mere *nullah*. Shamsuddin told her that during rainy season it was risky as the water almost touches the platform. However, people preferred living in these make shift structures as it was cheap.

"But it's illegal! Isn't it? " snapped Latika.

Shamsuddin laughed out. "What is legalized here? Nothing! We people of the slum are not even counted anywhere. They call us "Bangladeshi", illegal migrant. Nobody listens to us. We are poor and illiterate. We have to pay even for living here. What to do? Nobody cares for us. Whatever they say we do. "

"Who says?"

"Why? Everybody! The administration, police, the local goons, the colony people. Ask anybody and they will tell you everything about us without our consent. We cannot fight *Didi*. We are here to earn livelihood and as long as our family does not sleep empty stomach we are just about fine with it. "

They came across a narrow lane leading to the slum. Latika found both *kutcha* and nearly *pucca* houses on either side of the lane with their roofs almost touching each other. Shamsuddin led the way further into the slum where the lane was much narrower and the stench made it impossible to walk further. The narrow lanes filled with filth and over flowing drain. Latika was almost in tears to see the condition of people residing there. They were nothing short of an animal. Most of the children came out of their houses to see her. She looked like an alien in the community. Neatly dressed in an off white slawar kameez, her hair tucked in a bun on her nape, carrying a dairy in her hand she stood amid them as if from a different world. Her face had turned red with the sun blazing in the sky but her smile never faded from her lips. She looked at the children, filthy and almost naked staring at her. She bent down and asked for their name. They hesitated for a moment. Then she popped out some chocolates from her hand bag and offered them. In no time they grabbed it from her hand and ran away into hiding. The mothers came out to see who had offered the chocolates to their children. Latika walked up to the group of ladies staring at her.

She folded her hands and said "*Namskar Bidoh*! I am Latika."

But none of the ladies responded. They were too shy to say anything. Seeing Shamsuddin behind her they hurried indoors. Latika knew she had a big job ahead of her. Unlike Delhi the people here were more reserved and did not like much intrusion. She sighed and retraced her path.

"Shamsuddin is there some other entrance as well?" She asked.

"*Ho Didi*. It is on the farther side of the road," he answered walking ahead of her.

"Let's take that route. I want to see more of this place. Do you know this place well enough?" she asked.

"*Ho Didi*. Why not? I started from here. You will find people of different communities in the *basti*. Hindu, Bengali, Assamese, Muslim, Bihari you name it. And of course the *Miyan patti* which is on the other side of the Bharalu across the wooden bridge. Nobody prefers to go here due to the *Bangladeshi* tag.

"But the situation is so bad here. Doesn't anybody see to it?"

"Who is going to come here *Didi*? Nobody bothers for people like us. The most adjacent civilized society here is Kumhar para. That area is under municipal jurisdiction and has facilities like water supply, electricity and police. Our area is not counted under any wards. Most of the people residing in the slum are from far off villages and hardly notice anything bad. They are here to earn a livihood and that's all they care about," he briefed her.

Latika followed him quietly deep in her thought. She wondered how the volunteers worked here. She looked at her watch and saw that it was almost time to go back. The brief conversation with Shamshuddin told her a lot about the problem which persists in the area. She knew she is going to have a tough time ahead. Shortly they came across the other entrance and walked back to the car.

****

The nodal office had four employees who were responsible for the development work in the slum community at Kalapahar area. Debjyoti Bora, a man in his late thirties with an average height and well built physique, was the team leader. He was a computer programmer by profession and devoted his time entirely for the NGO activity in the area. He introduced Latika to his other team mates. Sachin Saikia was a PhD student who was doing his research on the urban slums of Guwahati. He came in contact with Debjyoti regarding his thesis and was very impressed by the social service his organisation was doing. He joined three years back. Prachi Ghosh was the youngest of them. She was only twenty four and almost a fresher. She joined them after completing her M.A in Sociology from Bangalore. Though her parents were against her joining the NGO as her merit could have earned her a much better job but Prachi preferred listening to her heart and once back from

Bangalore joined the NGO. Nayanmoni Pathak, the fourth person Latika was introduced to, was a lawyer by profession was responsible for increasing the network of the group. Through him lots of students, and professionals volunteered for the various projects of the NGO. He was sort of point of contact for the entire group. Everyone in the team had just one thing common and it was their passion of helping the underpreviledged. Latika was very happy to be one of them.

The next few days Latika teamed up with them to understand how they worked. She would visit the sites with them and hear them talk to the people in the local language. Interestingly every second lane had a different dilect in the slum community. The volunteers would also assist the activist in the visit and aware them about an upcoming health camp. Latika silently observed their work. She found that apart from language barrier she would also face the problem of mingling with the women folk. They were more reserved. They would not cooperate with the volunteers either.

Soon the day came when they were scheduled to organize the health camp. With Nayanmoni and Debjyoti's persuasion three doctors turned up to attend the camp. It was a non profitable organization so people associated voluntarily. Out of the three doctors one was a gynecologist and the other two were general physician. Although their team had put in all the efforts to make the people attend the camp but very few turned up. However not a single women turned up. Those visiting were mostly with the case of alcohol side effects. Latika was very sad with the statistics. She assumed good turn up after such a good campaign. But Debjyoti told her that this camp had been their best so far.

He told her that the people residing in this area were very conservative and equally illiterate and ignorant. They were more afraid to know that they may have certain disease and hence didn't turn up in the health camp. Unless they were real sick and could not afford the expenses of private clinics they won't turn up in the camp.

Latika understood that organizing a health camp without making the people aware of its benefit was a useless task. She jotted something down on her notepad to discuss later. Meantime, in the late evening when they were winding up, a woman turned up with her teenage daughter. The girl's age was not more than thirteen or fourteen years. The woman went to the gynecologist and narrated something to her about her daughter. The doctor conducted physical examination of the girl and asked the women to wait for a while. The doctor came out and discussed something with the other two doctors. The trio then called Debjyoti and Nayanmoni inside.

"This is a rape case," informed the lady doctor. "All the bruises in her private parts indicate something inhumane happened to her. Though her mother says she was beaten up and is here for some painkiller medicine. What do you think we should do?"

"Let's talk to the woman and see what she actually wants? Now since we know about it we must do something," Nayanmoni replied.

The lady doctor went inside and talked to the woman.

"Your daughter needs better medical attention. She is really suffering badly. You must admit her in the hospital immediately."

The woman hesitated and looked at her daughter. The girl started weeping.

The doctor consoled the girl saying, "I know what has happened to you and I am here to help you. So please tell me the truth."

"She fell off and got smacked. Nothing happened," snapped the woman wiping the sweat off her face with her sari. The girl looked at the woman and then at the doctor. Her weepy eyes kept crying for help yet the woman did not let her to get any. She only wanted some pain killers for her daughter.

The lady doctor looked up at Nayanmoni who was waiting outside. She shook her head. Nayanmoni understood that the woman would not confide anything at this moment. So he signaled the doctor to get done with the woman and he would take care of it later. The doctor prescribed some medicines and instructed the woman to contact her in case of any problem. The woman left with her daughter hurriedly.

The day had ended on a bad note. After the doctors left and the team sat down to analysis the situation. The camp turned out to be a failure. It did not attract much people and the last case was of more concern to them. The child needed medical attention but could not be provided because of the woman. There might be more such cases that go unreported. It was the major concern as it will urge the culprit to commit more crime. They sincerely searched for a solution for when Latika gave her opinion.

"I think we should target the women folk more as they are the prime victims. Our response has more or less been restricted to the men folk only. I think if we could break the barrier with these women then we can actually start at the ground level."

Debjyoti and Sachin agreed with her. Nayanmoni was more concerned about the number of women volunteers in their group. In all there were only four women including Latika and Prachi. Increasing their numbers can help their team reach out to more women in the slum area. They discussed over the matter but could not reach to any concrete conclusion. Finally they called off the day and returned home.

Chapter Nine

That night Latika spent the whole time tossing and turning in her bed. Every time she closed her eyes the girl's face would loom up before her eyes. Her teary eyes screaming for help. The girl had been in so much pain that she could barely walk. Yet knowing everything they could do nothing to help her. Latika made up her mind to help her anyhow. She tried to remember something about the woman which could help her trace the girl easily. Recalling the scenario she tried to figure out something about the woman which could give her a lead in tracing her. All she could remember was that she plump and stout drapped in a saree with glass bangles in her hands and no red *bindi* on her forehead. This clearly meant she was a Muslim woman. Latika at least knew where to lookout for the girl in the area and she needed Shamsuddin's help again. Most of the slum women set out to work early.

Early next morning she called up her aunt and asked her to convey a message to Shamsuddin. In about an hour Shamsuddin arrived in her place. Latika set out with him once more. She specifically asked him to take her to the Muslim dominated area in the slum community. Shamsuddin was puzzled as it was too early for someone like Latika to start her day. He did not say anything but lead the way quietly.

Once more Latika came to the place where she had come with Shamsuddin a few days earlier. This time the children were either sleeping or playing inside. Even the women were busy in their homes trying to finish off their chores before going to their job. Latika signaled Shamsuddin to go further. She was no more bothered about the nasty lane and stinky corners. She followed Shamsuddin while her eyes were looking out for the woman and girl who came to the camp in the evening. She kept on moving from one lane to the other without speaking anything. They reached the Bharalu after about an hour's walk.

The shops and stalls on the roadside beside the Bharalu were still closed. Only one tea stall was open. Latika asked Shamsuddin to stop for a while. She set down on a bench outside the tea stall and ordered for two cups of tea. Shamsuddin excused himself and went behind to smoke a *biri*. Latika scrutinized the surrounding. It was a small stall that also served homemade breakfast and snacks along with tea. The owner was an old man who ran the shop with his wife. It was not very difficult for Latika to make out that the old man was from Bihar as they usually have an ascent which makes them very distinct. She figured out that he might know people around as he also served food.

The old man stirred a spoon in the tea saucepan and the aroma of strong Assam Tea filled in the air. He crushed some cardamoms and a small chalk of ginger with a grinding stone and added it in the saucepan. A little later he added the milk and sugar. He stirred the spoon few more times in the mixture and covered the saucepan with a lid. Lowering the gas burner to low flame he picked two glasses from the bucket below and washed them with water. A little later he removed the lid and switched off the gas burner. The aroma of "masala" tea filled the surrounding. He carefully shifted the entire tea from the saucepan into an aluminum kettle through a filter and covered the lid of kettle. Then very precisely he filled up tea in the two glasses that he had washed earlier. He handed one glass to Latika and another to Shamsuddin.

Latika filled her lungs with the aroma first before sipping her tea. It was magical experience for her. After a long time she was drinking the flavored tea. It used to be her favorite beverage during her college days. She and her friends would sit and discuss variety of issues over masala tea in their college canteen. But the flavor got lost in her chase for big dreams. And today after many years reviving her taste bud she could not stop herself from appreciating the old man.

"*Baba*, it's very tasty. *Maza aa gaya*," she acclaimed sipping her tea. The old man smiled back.

He replied with pride, "You will not get this taste anywhere here. It is my special cut."

"Yes I could see that. It's just awesome," Latika agreed.

"My stall may be very small but I am doing this business for the last thirty years. Ask him?" He pointed out to Shamsuddin, "He is one of my old customers."

"*Ho. Chacha,*" Shamsuddin agreed.

"One who comes here and tastes my tea never forgets the taste," he added with pride.

"Then lots of people here must be your permanent customers," Latika asked.

"Yes many indeed. Mostly from the *basti,*" the old man replied.

"Then *Baba* you might know lots of people here?"

"Yes. I do."

"Do women also come here regularly." Her curiosity reached the peak.

He smiled hearing her question. "Why not? They drink tea too and eat the snacks. "

She hesitated for a moment. Then asked," I am looking for a Muslim woman." She described the woman and the girl.

"I might not be of much help in this. You can ask my wife as she is the one who sits in the evening mostly," he said.

"Can I meet her now?"

"Sure. Let me call her." The old man went behind the stall and came back with his wife.

"*Namaste Amma.* I am looking for a Muslim woman. Can you help me?" Latika asked.

The old lady thought for a moment then replied. "Most of the women come here in the evening for snacks on their way back to their home. I know many Muslim ladies by face. But I am not very sure about the one you are looking for. Why don't you come here in the evening? You might find her here. "

Latika thought about it. Of course she can come here. She thanked the old lady and rose to go.

"Ok. I shall come in the evening then," she said paying for the tea and left with Shamsuddin.

On their way back Shamsuddin asked her about the woman. She did not disclose him the reason but only described the woman physically. Shamshudin suggested her to visit Kumarpara where the women folk of the slum usually go to collect drinking water. She liked his suggestion and asked him to take her there.

****

They came by a primary school in Kumarpara. Just near the school boundary wall was a hand pump. Some "mekhla" clad women were filling water in their buckets and water pitcher.

Latika approached them with a smile. Though she looked like an outsider to them wearing jeans, kurti and a pair of sneakers but they did not hesitate to her advances. Instead they smiled back at her.

Latika was quite happy to get a positive response. She knew if she succeeded in building a rapport with these women then it would help her in her work. But she also knew that she was not very good at local Assamese language though she was learning it.

She tried her best in broken Assamese to make them understand that she was thirsty. The women understood and signed her to lower herself beneath the hand pump tap. She thanked them and did as was told. One of the women pumped the handle while Latika collected the flowing water into her palms and sipped it. After fulfilling her thirst she got up and wiped her lips with the back of her hands. She asked them with her little master over Assamese language if they came here every day. The women nodded.

"But then it's a long way you people come for water," Latika asked.

"What to do *Bidoh* there is no hand pump in our area and the well is dried up. So we have no option left but to come here," replied one of them.

"Oh!. It is really very difficult for you then," Latika said compassionately.

"We are poor people *Bidoh*. Who will listen to our woes?"

"Someone surely will. Soon things will change for better," Latika said.

The ladies looked at her with conviction and smiled.

She took their leave and walked up to Shamsuddin who had been watching her from a distance when she was speaking with the ladies.

"Your Assamese is too bad, *Didi*," he said smiling.

"What to do Shamsuddin? I hardly got a brush of it all these years," Latika said.

"It's easy *Didi*. You can easily learn it by practice."

"Ok then. From now on I shall speak with you in Assamese only. *Bujhisa Ne*?"

"*Hobo.*"

They returned back at Latika's house and Shamsuddin took her leave. Latika informed him that she would need his help more often during her visits in the slum area. He promised to escort her whenever needed and left.

****

Latika sat down on the verandah and fumbled with her shoe lace. The day was growing pretty hotter with every hour passing by. Her father came out and sat down with her.

"Where have you been so early in the morning?" he asked.

Latika had taken off her sneakers and was enjoying the feel of cool air in her feet.

"Just understanding the area *Bapi*," she answered. "I have to learn Assamese fast otherwise I will not be able to communicate properly with the people."

"You can start speaking with me from now onwards. It will take you sometime though to have the fluency but you must start now," her father replied.

After thinking a while her father added, "In our area people mostly speak Bengali and Assamese. Hindi is not a problem for you though you will find its usage pretty less in this area."

"Yes *Bapi*."

They sat there and drank tea before starting on with the day ahead.

Chapter Ten

Latika was finally assigned work by her team leader in the office. Her job was to interact with the women in the slum community and convince them to participate in the various educational camps in the area. It was a tough job but Debjyoti had faith in her capabilities.

Latika was very excited about her new assignment and wanted to prove herself in all possible ways. Though she knew with her lack of fluency in the local language it will be a big hurdle. She developed a habit of making a visit to the slum area every morning. It sort of boosted her confidence and moreover the chances of confronting women in the community were high compared in the later part of the day as they usually left for work. Moreover her urge to trace the Muslim woman was another major cause which she knew will not be possible with the team.

Shamsuddin always accompanied her during her morning visits which seemed more like morning walk to him but he didn't complaint. Before heading back they always stopped for tea at the small tea stall by the Bharalu. It was a routine that Shamsuddin enjoyed very much. He enjoyed answering her querries about the slum and liked listening to her various stories about the slum community in Delhi where she was working for the last couple of years. What surprised him mainly was with her caliber and education she was working for a community which no one ever bothers. He developed a great thinking for the people at the nodal office. Latika too learnt about the problems people faced in the village, sometimes due to flood, sometimes due to ethnic violence and sometimes due to militancy. What troubled her most was his community, even after so many generations of living in Assam, were considered as illegal migrants, the Bangladeshi, and there was nothing they could do about it other than bear the bruise. She empathized with him and promised herself to help him in all possible ways.

In the later part of the day, Latika would go again with her team of female volunteers and tried to contact as many women in the area. Sometimes the women folk responded otherwise most of the time they would run into hiding at the sight of the volunteers. Latika was enjoying the challenge.

****

So far she and her team had not succeeded in bonding with the women folk of the area. It was just limited to greetings and mere exchange of words. They were yet to come out of their shells but Latika waited patiently for them to confide in her. She believed sharing the extended help and education for which their NGO was working would be beneficial only when she won their trust. At least then the women would be ready to listen if not practice it. As for now their team was making themselves a known face in the area.

In few days time the women who earlier went into hiding seeing them now gained the confidence of confronting the team whenever they approached. The team's trail would often be followed by the young children who walked behind the volunteers from one lane to another. Surprisingly the volunteers found every second lane they had a different group of children trailing. Nevertheless, the volunteers enjoyed the children's presence during their visit in the slum. They would buy chocolates and cakes from the local shops for the children sometimes. Whereas the children readily vanished after grabbing it from their hands.

One day during one such visit, Latika disbursed chocolates to some children and they ran home as usual after grabbing it from her hand. A little later one of the children returned accompanied with a big girl.

"You want chocolates too," Latika asked.

The girl shook her head and asked Latika to come to her house. Latika and her other volunteer followed the girl. The girl took them to a house at the end of the lane. Latika asked the volunteer to wait outside while she went inside.

Once inside Latika had to first accustom her eyes to the darkness around. The house was a small dingy room with no provision for natural light. On one side was the kitchen area and on the other side of the room on the cot lay a woman whose body was a mere skeleton.

The girl said the woman on the cot was her mother who had been sick about a week. But she didn't have any money for her medicine and her father was a drunkard who would come home in the night and beat her for money. She also said that her mother worked as a maid and with her money the family earned a living. Now that her mother was sick so she was going to work in her mother's place. She said that she had asked for some monetary help from her employers but they said that her drunkard father had already collected her mother's salary in advance on the pretext of his wife's medication. The girl started weeping bitterly saying she did not want to lose her mother.

Latika consoled the girl and promised her all help. She asked her to bring the lamp so that she could see the woman lying on the cot clearly. In the light of the lamp Latika saw that the woman's face had gone pale and she was in a very critical state. She came out of the house and immediately called Sachin in the office. She informed him about the status of the woman and that she needed a lifting to the hospital immediately. Sachin promised to get back to her and hung off.

Meanwhile Latika explained to the girl that they will be admitting her mother in the hospital where all the medical expenses and investigations will be taken care of by her NGO. The girl sighed and hugged Latika. In a short time Sachin called up saying that Nayanmoni has arranged everything for the woman in the hospital and the ambulance was on the way. Now it was Latika's responsibility to take the woman to the ambulance as the vehicle could not enter the narrow lanes of the slum area.

Latika knew she had to arrange for a hand cart or some other means to carry the woman out of the narrow lane to the ambulance waiting outside. She found a man with a hand cart and asked him to help her. With his help she shifted the ailing woman from the cot to the cart and then to the ambulance waiting on the road. The girl escorted her mother to the hospital where Nayanmoni was waiting for them.

The entire episode was watched by the people in the area. When Latika came back to the lane to join her volunteer who was at that time taking care of the young child left behind she was amazed to see the women speaking to the volunteer. When they saw Latika they appreciated their effort for saving the woman.

It was a day Latika could never forget as this small incident gave her a major breakthrough in her mission which she had been trying to do for the last couple of months. From that day onwards people in the area thought of team as God send angels who were devoting time to help them instead.

Latika was specially approached by the woman folk and they lovingly called her Latika *Bidoh*. They loved to share their happiness and problems with her without any hesitation. Thus from that day onwards the team started to work with full cooperation from the locals.

In few days the woman whom Latika had admitted in the hospital came home. She had regained much of her lost strength and looked healthier. The doctor had advised her bed rest for few weeks before she could resume her work. Latika made a point to visit her many often to inquire about her well being. The woman recovered faster than Latika had thought.

One day when Latika went to meet the woman, she shared her desire to educate her children. She said although she was illiterate but she knew through education alone she can give a better life to her daughters. Latika was very happy to learn about it. At least here was one woman who did not want her girls to do what she was doing. She assured the lady that she would discuss about it with her team.

So far the team of volunteers only emphasized on health and hygiene programs in the community. But now the women seem to show interest in their overall development as well. It was a good sign. They now started providing elementary education to the community children. In less than a month's time after the incident Latika became a well known face in the area. She mostly worked with the women welfare and thus became a popular figure among the women in the slum.

****

Latika was riding high the waves of her success. She had successfully started the welfare project in a small portion of the slum community. Days passed by and Latika and her team made a good progress. Debjyoti and Nayanmoni although were very impressed with her work however, their concern was Latika's changing behavior. With each added feather in her cap Latika's attitude transformed. She was egoistic and proud. She even started taking her own decisions irrespective of its consequences. She didn't like anybody questioning or giving advice. Whatever she thought she considered it to be always correct. Many a times she ventured out with her team in unassigned areas without informing the office. Her attitude made it uneasy for the volunteers to work with her as she would always keep pushing them for results. But that didn't affect Latika.

Sachin and Prachi hinted her many times but Latika didn't listen. She would rather say, "It's my way or highway!"

****

One day, Latika and her team were having tea in the old man's small tea stall before returning to the office. They were in a middle of discussion when they heard two guys calling names to the old man. Latika looked up and saw them. They were in their early twenties, lanky with long hair that reached their shoulders, ears pierced and the buttons of their shirt all open.

They looked anything but decent. They tore open the jar of sweet candies on the counter and took out a handful of it. When the old man tried to stop them they started calling him names once again and left without paying anything.

Latika asked the old man about the guys. He told her that they belonged to Deka's gang. So far Latika and her team had not crossed paths with these guys and hence knew nothing about them. She asked the old man to elaborate further.

He said that Deka headed a gang of local goons who made their living mostly by extortion from local shops in the area. The people willingly or unwillingly parted with a small amount according to their income just to avoid their shops getting vandalized by these people. He told her that these people were also quite renowned for their criminal activities in Kalapahar and the police kept a tight vigil on them. However, since the slum had least police protections these people do away with whatever they wanted. He even alerted Latika to keep a safe distance from them. Latika thanked the old man for the advice and left with her team.

The next day when they started work they found the same guys trailing them. Initially she thought it might be a sheer coincidence but they started passing lewd comments at one of her volunteers Latika could not stop herself. She went out straight to them and gave them some piece of her mind and warned them. For few seconds they could not understand what was going on. Nobody ever had guts to talk to them like that in the locality. They were taken by surprise but later laughed out.

"Do you know who we are?" said one of them.

"No, I don't want to. I am only asking you to leave and let us work." Latika snapped crossing her arms across her chest.

One of them roved his eyes over her body saying, "How come honey we missed you. You should...."

Before he could complete Latika slapped him hard enough that made him lose his balance and send him fumbling for support.

The guy straightened himself up while his hand still covered his cheek which she had slapped. He saw crowd gathering and knew well his repute was at stake. He hurled himself at Latika but she ducked swiftly. Her karate lessons in college helped her. The guy lost his balance this time and tumbled down in the pool of mud water.

The other guy rushed for his help but the onlookers laughed out. The guys could take no more insult and took to their feet. They heard people clapping behind as they walked away. Latika and her team went back to work without thinking much about it.

Later in the evening one of girls narrated the incident of the day to Debjyoti. Being a local he knew Deka too well to stake his repute at the hands of a woman. Debjyoti sensed the danger and immediately updated Nayanmoni about it. Meanwhile he asked Latika to come to his cabin and tried putting some sense in her.

"Did you venture in unassigned area today?" he asked.

"Since when did you start questioning me about it?" she answered with an attitude.

"Latika, you cannot do away with it every time. I did not reason earlier because I didn't know about it," he said.

"I didn't know I had to inform you about my every action," she said angrily.

"I never doubted your abilities, Latika. But you cannot risk others life with your impulsive decisions." His voice was calm.

"Risking life? What do you mean?"

"Why? Didn't you put up a fight today?"

"I taught him a lesson!" she corrected.

"You knew well he was a member of Dekka's gang and you were with only female volunteers. God forbid if something happened to any of them who would be responsible, Latika? " he demanded.

"How can you ignore someone constantly bugging you at your work? I cannot do that. That volunteer was my responsibility and I would not let anybody harm her reputation." She fumed at him.

"Latika, are you saying I don't care about my people?" Debjyoti asked calmly.

"No. I did not mean that. But I did not expect you to say such a thing either?" Latika was still angry.

"Fine if you think what you did today was the right then so be it. Next day somebody smacks someone I still keep cool. Instead of social service let's start karate classes here," said Debjyoti raising his voice slightly but still maintaining his calm. "What should I do if God forsaken something happens in the field which we cannot abate? You could have informed Nayan or me and we could have taken care of it."

"I disagree. I cannot keep mum when something is wrong in front of my eyes. I call a spade a spade when it needs to be. " Latika snapped.

"Fine then I shall not be responsible for whatever happens in future. You face it yourself," he replied with his tone unchanged.

"Thanks for showing me the way." Latika burst with anger. She turned abruptly and walked out of his office closing the door behind her. She picked up her hand bag from her seat and left without saying a word to anyone.

Debjyoti sat back in his chair. He could not believe what he just heard. He had tried to warn her but she did not listen. He hid his face in his palms and let out a deep sigh.

Chapter Eleven

The next day Latika did not go to work. The argument with Debjyoti was too disturbing for her. She disliked the very thought that a man could stake a woman's modesty so easily. It never crossed her mind that he was simply warning her against the local goons. She was too much imposed in her false arrogance to listen to anyone. She felt very lonely. For the first time in almost a year she felt she had made a wrong decision to come to Guwahati. Suddenly she felt the people were too cold to stir a change. Everything about the place was slow. The learning, the progress, the delivery was slow. She hated the whole system here. People were too weak to confront a branded criminal and she simply could not digest it.

The whole day she spent in the house sat watching TV and reading newspaper. In the evening she went out to meet her aunt, Snehlata. She saw her packing clothes in a bag.

"Where you are going, *Pishi*?" Latika asked.

"I am going to Shillong for few days to beat the heat. Your *Pisha* has been to Mumbai for two weeks and I thought of taking some time out with myself. You want to come along?" asked Snehlata.

Latika accepted the invitation. She went back home and started packing her bag. She was not sure what kind of clothes to pack, summer wear or warm clothing. She put in a pair of jeans and couple of sweat shirts. In about an hour she was back at Snehlata's place.

A cab was already waiting outside the house. Latika loaded the luggage in the cab and waited outside for her aunt. Snehlata handed the house keys to Shamsuddin and instructed him to take care of the house and cattles in her absence. The cab drove away towards the busy main road.

Shillong, the capital of Meghalaya, was the nearest hill station and about four hours drive from Guwahati. Their cab took the highway and it swept past the hills and valleys up in mountain. The serpent like road and the stunning scenery around thrilled Latika very much. She was going to Shillong after almost two decades. She use to make visit there sometimes as a kid with her parents but after shifting to Delhi she hardly had enough time to visit this beautiful hill station. She never knew how much she had yearned for this trip.

Also her argument with Debjyoti the previous day had drained her out completely and she needed a break badly. She listened to old Hindi movie songs as their cab swept past the pine trees along the sides of the hills. The sun was down already by the time they reached Nongpoh. They took a small tea break and moved on. It was late evening when they finally reached Shillong. Latika was completely relaxed by the time she reached the city

They drove past the busy roads across the city on the outskirts. The cab finally stopped in front of a small cottage uphill away from the main city. It was Snehlata's summer house.

Earlier the whole family use to spend their summer vacation here. But the children were now married and settled in other cities. It was just Snehlata who visited regularly every year either alone or sometimes with her husband.

Snehlata paid the driver and got down first. She opened the small gate with a spare key and waited for Latika who unloaded their bags from the cab. The cab left as they climbed the stairs to the front verandah.

Seeing the entrance lights on Latika asked if someone was inside the house. Snehlata said that the care taker must have left them open as she had informed her about their arrival late in the evening. The verandah had wooden flooring and fencing. Just besides the fencing were numerous plants tubs. Snehlata bent down and picked up a hidden key among the plant tubs. She opened the lock of the front door with the key and went inside.

The cottage lit up brilliantly with lights as Snehlata put on the main switch. It was a cozy little cottage with single room accommodation. But it was spacious with an open kitchen on one side and sleep area on the other side. The sleep area had two single bed separated by a night table. The two portion of the room was separated by a wide passage that led to the back door. Latika put down the luggage in the passage and took a good look at the room.

It had been two decades since she last came to the house. A family picture on the night table caught her attention. She walked up and took a close look at the picture. It was an old family picture. Latika kept it down carefully.

"You have lots of memory with this place, *Pishi*," she asked her aunt.

Snehlata opened the back door and let in the fresh air. "Yes. This house is our anniversary gift and I always love it. One day I shall shift here permanently. I like it here better than anywhere else," she answered.

Latika sat down on the bed and scrutinized the room. Adjacent to the front doors were two big glass windows that overlooked the front verandah. The room had a small study table and another served as fine dining for two in the name of furniture. Both the tables were placed near the window to give a good glimpse of the view outside.

Latika got up from the bed and went to check the back door. It opened to a small gallery at the end of which was the toilet and a small changing room adjacent to it. It had a wardrobe and a full length mirror.

"It's beautiful *Pishi*. I wonder why I didn't come here earlier!" exclaimed Latika.

Snehlata was unpacking her bag in the changing room. "You think so?"

"Yes. I mean it. See the place has limited things yet it's sufficient. I love it," Latika replied excitedly.

"Then you wait till the morning. You will like it more at sunrise," said Snehlata.

"Is it? Then I am already off to bed," giggled Latika.

They quickly freshen up and had their dinner of boiled potato and butter with hot rice. It was the fastest dish which could be cooked without any preparation. It could be garnished with green peas, green chilies and chopped onions. And not to mention a bowl of boiled *Masoor dal*.

However this time Snehlata and Latika had to minus the rest of garnishing from their plate as it was already 10.00 pm and almost midnight in Shillong. Roads were empty, shops closed and people were already indoors calling off the day. Latika changed into her track pants and tees and curled inside the blanket in her bed. Her bed was just adjoining the window on the side wall of the room that overlooking the hills.

She clutched the corner of the curtain and shove it aside a little to take a glimpse of the world outside. The naked darkness and the howling of dogs outside prompted her duck under the blanket. In no time she was asleep. That night she slept peacefully forgetting everything.

The sun peeked into her bed through the window as Latika slowly opened her eyes in the morning the next day. She slightly tilted up her head from the pillow and shoved the curtain of the window once again. The beauty outside was enchanting. Pine trees swayed slowly as the wind blew towards the slopes of the hills. At the far distance the road glistened in the sun like the tail of a serpent. It was the most beautiful morning she had ever seen. She climbed down from her bed and found her aunt, Snehlata, already up. She was sitting outside in the verandah stairs enjoying the morning along with her cup of red tea.

"You don't get up so late in the hills. I have already taken a stroll and now sipping my tea," said Snehlata as she heard Latika.

Latika popped her head out of the door and replied, "Yes *Pishi*, I will from tomorrow. It is so beautiful out here. I now remember I use to come here sometimes with dad in my childhood but it had been a long time since. Thanks for bringing me along. I needed this break badly," she said.

A little later Latika too sat down on the stairs of the verandah beside her aunt and enjoyed the morning aura of this beautiful place. Both sat in silence engulfed in their own thoughts. Only the sound of sipping tea was heard sometimes. They sat like that for some time holding the warm cup in between their palms as if draining all the warmth from the chinaware into their blood. Back home their morning was more of a routine chore which they had to follow without wasting any time to avoid getting late. Snehlata had to take care of her family and Latika had to catch up with her office. So enjoying an early morning at leisure was almost left out. But here the time had stopped counting for them. Everything was left behind to only beautiful serene ambiance in the lap of nature.

Snehlata broke the silence. "You know Latika, my father use to say Shillong has the most beautiful mornings. And to realize that it took me sixty long years. As a child I was busy raising the siblings and then busy as a mother. So actually I never got time to spend for myself. But now when children have grown up and don't need me anymore I take out time and come here many often. I wish your *Pisha* could take out some time as well. His work keeps him very busy. "

"Yes *Pishi*. He is really busy man but then it is good for his health too at this age. Touch wood he is hale and hearty as ever," Latika replied.

"So what are your plans for today?"

"May be I will just laze around. Nothing in particular though," Latika answered.

"Well then we can go and meet my childhood friend."

"Your childhood friend??" Latika exclaimed. "That will be great."

They had a quick breakfast of toast with jam and butter along with egg poaches followed by a cup of red tea. Then they set off. Before leaving Snehlata once again left the keys in the specific place for her caretaker who would come in the scheduled time later to do the cleaning.

Since the cottage was uphill they had to walk till the main road all the way downhill to catch a taxi. The walk after the quick breakfast was more fun as the sun was more merciful here than in Guwahti at this time of the day and the ambiance awesome to distract all the pain if any.

Chapter Twelve

They took a taxi and after about an hour's drive reached their destination on another hill top on the end of the city. They got down in the small market place of the locality and went inside a fruit shop. Snehlata bought some selected fruits and asked the lady to gift wrap them in a fruit basket. Then she went inside a sweet shop and ordered a packet of Bengali *Sandesh*. She handed the packet to Latika and took the fruit basket in her hand and walked out of the shop.

From the market place they again walked a little uphill towards the residential area of the locality. It was a narrow foot lane with beautiful cottages on both sides. All the houses were of Assam style with tin roof and numerous glass windows on all sides to capture maximum natural light. Each house had a stretch of green lawn in the front with a beautiful flower garden to enhance the front view. Latika was very excited to see them. She fidgeted like a little girl following Snehalat all the way till the end of the lane.

Snehlata finally stopped in front of a house with white walls and red tin sheets. The main verandah of the house like Snehlata's too had a wooden fencing and a small wooden gate. The house was separated from the main gate on the road by a stretch of small green lawn in between. From the main gate of the house a narrow cemented passage led to the verandah steps.

Snehlata opened the latch of the main gate and went inside. Latika followed behind closing the gate back once again. They walked on the passage and reached the steps leading to the front verandah. Snehlata searched for the call bell when the front door opened and an old lady clad in a crumpled white sari that matched her grey hair came out. Her face was spotlessly fair and her eyes a total contrast to her skin. They matched the color of charcoal. Even at this age she was awesomely beautiful. Seeing Snehlata she ran down the steps and gave a tight hug. Then she took them indoors.

The lady did not stop in the drawing room instead took her guests straight to her kitchen which was at the end of the verandah. It was a big hall with a small coffee table near the window that overlooked the main gate of the house. She asked her guest to ease themselves while she went to one of the kitchen shelves and returned with a betel- nut box.

She placed the betel box on the table in front of Snehlata and handed her a finely cut betel leaf. Snehlata took the leaf from her hand and placed it carefully over the betel nut box. The lady sat across another chair at the coffee table facing Snehlata. Her smile never faded from her face. For some minutes both looked at each other smiling. The other lady looked much older than Snehlata yet she was very beautiful.

"It's so good to see you, Lata, after such a long time," said the lady patting Snehlata's hand.

"Same here, Monidi. How have you been all the while?" asked Snehlata patting the lady's hand in return.

Glad with Snehlata's gesture the lady pulled across her hand from the table and replied, "Good. As long as I am able to take care of myself I have nothing to worry." She paused then said, "People are so much busy with their life today that they hardly have time for an old woman like me. If something happens and I am bedridden I shall die that very day." Her tone was heavy.

"Why do you think like this, Monidi. God will always take good care of you," Snehlata tried to cheering her up. "Here meet Latika, my younger brother's daughter."

Latika got up from the chair and went up to the lady. She bent down and touched the lady's feet as an old tradition in India where the younger ones touch the elder's feet and take their blessings as a sign of salutation.

The lady patted Latika's shoulders and searched for Latika's eyes. Latika smiled back at her. Then getting up Latika went to Snehlata and touched her feet as well as. Then she took seat in the chair.

"Oh! She has grown up into a lovely woman", exclaimed the lady. "Do you remember you use to visit our home sometimes with your father when you were young?"

Latika blushed up a little and shook her head.

"How is your father, sweetie?" asked the lady.

"He is fine," answered Latika.

"She has finally come to serve her father. Now onwards she will be staying in Guwahati," added Snehlata.

"Oh! That's good news," said Monidi. She turned to Latika and said, "After your mother's demise he always wanted you near him. He felt so lonely. It's good that you have taken this decision." She paused then looking away continued," Parents do a lot for their children but when they grow up they forget everything. Just see my condition. I have raised my sons all by myself. Your uncle had expired long time ago. My sons were kids then. I had nothing left but this house only. But I gave them good education because of which they have a good life today. But nothing has changed for me. I am still where I had always been, alone and old. " A tear dropped down from her eyes as she concluded. She wiped with the corner of her sari.

Snehlata tried to console the lady saying, "Monidi, you cannot blame them. Life is different today. See, my children have also left to seek out a future for them. If they don't then all their education and our efforts will be futile. I am happy for them and you too should be happy about them."

Latika sat quietly in her chair listening everything. Surely she too had been neglecting her parent's side for the sake of her career so long. Never once did she think about them or understood that every time they gave her permission to go ahead they were pushed behind a little more in her life.

The old lady composed herself and said, "I am sorry ladies. It's just that you don't discuss your heart out to just anyone. Lata you make me cry every time you visit." Then she looked at Latika lovingly and asked, "Ok now you tell me what you would like to have?"

"We got something for you aunty." Latika said handing the fruit basket and packet of sweet to the old lady.

"Oh that's so sweet of you. Let me see what I got here," said the old lady. She opened up the packet of sweet and the fruit basket and then brought two plates from the shelf. She picked two sandesh from the packet and kept each one of it on the plate. Then she served the plates to Latika and Snehlata. She once again went back to the shelf to bring a fruit knife.

Placing the fruit knife on the coffee table she said, "Please help yourself while I make you some tea."

"No Monidi you please sit. Latika will make tea," said Snehlata.

"No. That's ok. Let her enjoy. I will make you one right away." She did not wait for any answer instead went to the kitchen area on the other side of the hall and started preparing tea.

Snehlata watched the old lady at work. Their plates lay untouched. Latika picked up an apple from the basket and went to the sink to wash it. She came back again and started peeling off the skin of the apple with the knife.

Snehlata shifted her gaze from the old lady to Latika. After finishing off Latika sliced the apple into several pieces and placed them on her plate beside the sandesh. By that time the old lady also joined them with three cups of tea and a jar of cookies. She placed them on the table and went back to get a plate. She picked up some cookies out of the jar and served them on the plate. Then she too sat down on her chair by the table.

Latika picked up a cookie from the plate and took a bite. It melted in her mouth leaving a distinct sweet-salty taste. "Wow! It's delicious." She said.

"It's Monidi's patent cookies," said Snehlata. "You will not get this flavor anywhere else. I have been after her life for so many years for the recipe but she won't give me."

The old lady laughed out and said, "Before I close my eyes forever Lata, I shall give you the recipe. Till then you enjoy it from my hands."

Both Snehlata and Litika laughed out loud.

"Remember those days Monidi when we were neighbors. You were a new bride then and always kept a veil and my brothers would jump up the wall of your kitchen to have a glimpse of you." Snehlata said.

"And I had to always keep the windows of the kitchen closed because of them no matter how suffocating it was. And……."

The ladies did not stop after that. They had so much to catch up with after so many days that Latika's presence was almost nonexistent to them. She quietly finished her tea and got up from the chair to leave them alone for some time in their gossip.

Chapter Thirteen

She went out to the front verandah to take a good view. The highest view point of the city, The Shillong Peak, was clearly visible from the place where she stood. The clouds dancing to the tunes of the wind blowing high up in the mountains made a spectacular sight. The day was bright and sunny yet the weather was cool. Latika inhaled lung full of air stretching her arms as if she wanted to pin the picture in her mind for ever. She stood there for some moments and thought people would be fool to stay away from a place like this.

Slowly her interest averted to the other side of the house. She took a turn along the verandah and reached the back side of the house. It had a small court yard and an outhouse at the other end. She walked down the steps of the verandah and crossing the court yard stood in front of the outhouse. Unlike the main house it was very old.

The walls of the outhouse were of mud and the roof was made of very small tin sheets joined together. Also the doors and windows of the house had wooden panes instead of glass unlike the other houses. Even the latch on the main door was a small iron chain that was simply attached to a hook on the top of the door frame. The door was not locked so Latika easily unleashed the chain and threw open the door.

It was a very small room and the walls were hand painted in white. The flooring was also of mud that was neatly mopped. The room had a small old wooden circular table and an arm chair in the name of furniture. There were two small rooms attached on each side of the main room. One was dumped with trash and looked like a store while the other was nicely decorated and had a small temple in the middle with idols of Lord Krishna and Radha.

Latika closed her palms together and bowed down to the deity. Then she came out of the house and closed the door. She leashed the chain of the door once again and walked up to the verandah inside the house. On her way back to the hall where the ladies sat she scrutinized the interior of house. She found several rooms in the passage that led to the hall. As the doors of the rooms were wide open she peeked inside. The rooms were small but cozy and each displayed the taste of its owner. She could easily make out which one was son's and daughter's room. One room was larger than the rest and had a TV set. The walls of this room were adorned with calendars pictures of various deities. She could make out it was the master bedroom.

She went back to the ladies and took her seat once again. The ladies looked up at her and asked about her whereabouts. She told them she was exploring the premises.

She even complimented the old lady for her beautiful temple in the outhouse.

"This was all I could bring here with me at that time," replied the old lady replied. Her eyes were once again glistening with tears as the remembered her past. She paused for a moment then resumed the conversation," Your Uncle's great grandfather was a very renowned man in the then East Bengal. Our family was counted among one of the prominent families in that area but nothing counted that fateful night when the entire village was torched by the rioters. We fled with whatever we could lay our hands upon. We knew nobody in India except your grandfather. So we came here. I was just thirteen then newly married. We stayed in your grandfather's house for about six months then shifted into this house. The outhouse you saw at the backyard is our original house. We were total fifteen family members and all stayed in that small house for years. This house that you are sitting now was built much later by my late father-in-law but he did not allow any changes in the old house. Apart from small fixings nothing has been changed in it so far. It as it is, a living example of our awful days."

She paused again and turned to Snehlata, "If your father had not supported us we would have been dead long back." She wiped off a tear drop from the corner of her eyes with her saree again.

"Even today I bear the pain when I see these empty rooms. When my father-in-law built this house he had only one thought in mind that his children should not suffer which he and his siblings had to go through. But see, none of them are here to even light an oil lamp in front of the deity. I wonder what will happen when I close my eyes someday."

"Monidi why do you always think like that," asked Snehalata.

"It's because to make this house a home I and my father-in-law have put in lots of efforts. But I know what my children and others will do the moment I die. They will sell it off and return back to their lives as if nothing mattered. They are ready to struggle and start from a scratch in a new city rather than cherish with what they have in a known place. They are least interested in preserving the legacy and will turn up as a struggler just like their forefather. But it will not end there. Their children will also follow their parent's steps in near future and leave them to fend alone in their old age. So ultimately, you see, the family will have no roots, no legacy. This is what I fear most. After losing everything in partition we have taken great pains in preserving our culture and roots. But today's generation hardly takes notice of our pain. For them their career is everything and they even don't mind being rootless. What kind of life are they going to give to the future generation?"

Her fear was true. This is what has been happening around. People are moving out of joint families and starting a nuclear family. Their world is crumbling down to "I, me and myself" phase. Gone are the days when a house would light up to the laughter of children, grandparents, uncles and aunties from morning till night. Each member shared the joy and sorrow of the family together. Life was easier and stress free unlike today. Of course the financial crunch was always there but then there were so many shoulders to share the weight.

Latika remembered her own life in Delhi. In spite of a promising career her personal life was jeopardize. No matter how mature and independent woman she thought she was but she could not handle her own marriage issues that ended in divorce. Monidi's statement made her thought if the situation would have been different had she been with family instead. At least there would have been emotional support if not anything else. Her life rocked as long as she stood strong but the moment she trembled it blew her off altogether. It took her considerable time to reconcile herself once more and she came out strong. She was pretty happy with what she decided to do now.

But the thoughts made her realize that she was not doing what she should have been doing at the moment. Leaving her job she was spending time at a hill station listening to a destitude old lady. Was this what she wanted in her life? Where is her dedication? Her thoughts provoked her to call up her office and tell them that she would be taking few days off from work. She excused herself went out to check her mobile.

The call log showed neither any call nor any message from her office. It troubled her. She realized she had been very rude the other day and repented badly. She came back to the ladies inside but this time her mind strayed elsewhere. She was very disturbed.

They spent the day at Monidi's house and returned to their cottage in the evening. Snehlata sensed something troubling Latika but waited for an appropriate time. Later when they sat down to relax Snehlata asked Latika about her problem. Initially Latika denied but when Snehlata insisted she broke down. She narrated the whole incident at her office the other day. Snehlata listened without interrupting.

"I don't know what to do, *Pishi*?" sobbed Latika.

"Do you have Debjyoti's number?" her aunt asked.

Latika nodded.

"Then don't wait. Give him a call," Snehlata suggested.

Latika hesitated. Then replied, "But *Pishi* I don't know how he will react?"

"Fine!" said her aunt. "Keep brooding then for the rest of the days ahead. But remember you have to face him once you go back. And it's never late to apologise."

Latika did not answer and dug under her blanket. Darkness engulfed her as she opened her eyes underneath the blanket. She fought hard thinking of ways to start conversation with Debjyoti. She kept rehearsing the lines in her mind that she wanted to say but it didn't seem appropriate to her. She wanted to start with something that looked casual and not intervening. Digging hard in her mind she gave up and closed down her eyes.

Next day Snehlata informed her that she was going to visit her sister-in-law. Latika gave the invitation a pass. She would tour the city instead she thought. Snehlata reminded her to be home in time and left. Latika crawled in the bed once more. She had a long day ahead and figured out how to kick start it. Somewhere in her mind the previous day's conversation with Monidi was ringing in her mind. The thought of leaving her father alone in the house too bothered her. Overall she was in a confused state of mind and didn't know what to do.

An hour later the care taker came to do her usual chore in the house. She was an old Nepali lady. She greeted Latika with a big grin and asked if she wanted anything. Latika smiled back and shook her head. The lady started her work and Latika had no option but to get out of her bed. She was still in her night gear, track pant and tee.

Slipping the flip flop in her feet she headed for the verandah. The road ahead looked inviting. She opened the gates and stepped on the street. It was empty as long as her eyes could search. She thought of exploring uphill and started walking lost in her own thoughts. At the blind turn of the road she heard someone playing guitar. She looked up towards the source of the sound. It was coming from the bunglow a little up hill off the side of the road from where she stood. A small hoarding indicated that it was a guest house. A narrow dirt road off the main road led to the entrance of the guest house at the far end. She left the trail of the main road and took the dirt road. With each step towards big iron gates she felt a strange excitement growing within her. The sound of the guitar was still loud and clear as she walked towards the iron gates.

The gates were wide open so she walked into the premises. The beauty was enchanting. Grooves of pine trees encircled the bunglow giving it a very serene and spectacular look. Latika was tempted to go inside but the sound of guitar was too intervening to think of anything else. She walked down slowly towards it down the big verandah.

A group of boys were lazing in the sun sitting under a pine tree. One of them saw her and alerted others. They waved at her with a smile. The one playing the guitar had his back on her. He turned back to see who his friends were waving at. Seeing Latika he jumped up on his feet. Latika was equally surprised looking at him.

Chapter Fourteen

Debjyoti was surprised to see Latika standing in front of him. It took him some moments to sink in the realty. Then he too waved at her.

"What are You doing here?" Latika asked without waiting for him to question anything. Her eyes were big as saucer unable to believe what they saw.

Debjyoti was by now use to her tone of questioning. Her bewildered looks amused him. He handed the guitar to one of his friends and came up to her. Latika still had the puzzled look on her face.

"Why? This happens to be my uncle's place and I am just chilling out with my friends." He replied with a smile.

"No but….Oh. Ok. Hi." Latika had hard time digesting the fact. Not about whom this premises belonged to but rather seeing Debjyoti in front of her.

"Hello." His eyes never left hers as he greeted her and continued, "How come you are here?"

"I came here with my aunt. She owns a cottage just down the road," Latika answered.

"Oh that's good. We got neighbors then. Well I come here sometimes on weekend. I like it here. You can say it's my stress buster. The other day somebody gave me a very hard time so I had no option but to run for cover here." He said teasingly.

Latika did not waste a second understanding what he meant. She immediately apologized to him about her abrupt behavior the other day and also for not informing the office about her absence from work.

Debjyoti nodded slightly but didn't say anything. But Latika felt the load off her shoulders. It was so easy she thought and none of her rehearsed lines came to her rescue. The words just dropped out of her mouth and she felt relieved.

Debjyoti took note of her easiness and asked smiling, "Any plans for today."

Latika shrugged. "Actually no. My aunt left to visit some kin so I was wondering what to do? "

"Well, you can join us if you want to. We are heading for a trek among the hills. Will be back by evening." He suggested.

Latika was not sure what to say but nodded instead.

"Well then I give you twenty minutes to get ready. By that time our pack lunch will also be ready. We shall meet here then."

"Ok."

She returned to her cottage and got ready within minutes. She quickly dumped a bottle of water and some packets of biscuits and namkeen in her backpack and went out to meet the boys in the guest house. On the way she tried to call up Snehlata to inform her about her plan but the line did not go through. She thought of catching up with her later. She was so excited that she could sense butterflies in her stomach but wondered whether it was due to meeting Debjyoti or going for a trek. It had been ages since she last went for camping to Jim Corbert with her friends. Either way her excitement was at peak.

They left the guest house with packed lunch and headed for the hills at the backside of the guest house. In few minutes they left all the human habitation behind and walked past the hilly terrain among the pine groves. Debjyoti was leading the track while Latika was the last person to follow. The guys were having fun cracking jokes and singing some old Bollywood tunes while checking on Latika in between to see if she was fine.

They finally reached a stream after walking for about two hours. The water was cold and crystal clear. Debjyoti stopped and so did others.

"We rest here guys. Is it ok?" He asked turning back.

The guys had already taken off their back pack and were anxious to take a plunge in the running water. Latika looked up at Debjyoti. He understood what she meant.

"We will rest here. So you can relax now." He confirmed.

Latika put down her back pack. She looked for a clean place to sit. Soon the guys joined her. She took out the packet of biscuit and namkeen from her bag and offered them. They shared it and returned her back. Debjyoti came over and introduced his friends to her. They were total five of which two were his cousins. They left for a dip in the stream leaving Debjyoti and Latika behind.

"I didn't know you play guitar so good." Latika said.

"Music is part of life in the hills. We are born with it. You see Hemanta," he said pointing towards the lean and tall guy with long hair, "He has his own band. You should hear him play someday. He is a genius."

"That's nice to hear. So you guys often go for trekking." She asked quite eagerly.

"Yeah sometimes. It is never organized. Whenever I come we make up some trip or go camping." He rested on his elbow on the grass and gazed at her.

Latika shoved aside a strand of her hair off her eyes and met his gaze. "Had I not met you here I would not have known so many different attributes of yours." She said smiling.

He laughed. "Yeah it's a sheer coincidence that we met here. Actually I was wondering why you did not turn up in the office the other day. I asked everybody in the office but nobody knew. But I had no idea that I would meet you here." He sounded excited.

"Actually I was trying to call you up to apologize but didn't know how to start. Sometimes I am very bad at facing people you know. But I thank god that I tumble upon you this morning otherwise it would have been bugging me inside the whole time I am here." She disclosed.

"You don't have to think that way. Even I think I could not handle the situation properly that day so I annoyed you. Actually Dekka is a renowned criminal. And I didn't want any harm upon the team for any reason whatsoever.

I had already informed Nayanmoni about it and he said he had updated the police about it but then it is better to take precaution from our end. " He informed her.

"I understand."

"In fact after that day we had made it compulsory that none of the lady volunteers will venture alone. Also every team will have male volunteers for visit in the slum area."

"I think that's a good idea."

"In your absence Prachi has been assigned the team responsibility. And you know she is quite excited about it. I just hope she does well to her role. You have done too good a job. Everyone appreciates that. I hope you have no more qualms and will join us soon." His question was direct.

Latika hesitated for a moment. "Did he think I will not join?" She thought then nodded her head.

Debjyoti sighed out a relief and got up to join his buddies in the running stream. Latika lay on her back on the grass and stretched her legs while the guys had fun in the water. Latika heard them shouting and calling names at each other. They invited her too to join them but she refused them politely.

She did not think it proper to jump in water with strangers no matter how promising the water looked. She knew it had taken her lot of deliberation to come and join them for a trek. Even though she had said "Yes" to Debjyoti in the guest house but when she returned home to change she was in a dilemma whether to go or not. She finally made up her mind to give it a go and was glad that she had taken the decision. It was a pleasant day and lying on the ground she was enjoying the moment of her life.

When the boys were finally exhausted and hungry they came out of water and dressed up. They joined Latika under the shade of the tree and relaxed. Hemanta unpacked the lunch which they had brought from the guest house and Latika served it to everybody. After lunch Hemanta hummed to the tunes of Kishore Kumar and Md. Raffi to jazz up the environment. Finally they headed for the pavilion.

On the way back Debjoyti walked by Latika's side. They discussed on variety of topics and interests. Anything from work was on their conversation list. They discussed on movies, books, sports, food just about anything that made their life. In a way they got to know each other better than at work. They reached the guest house just before sun down. Latika thanked all the guys for a wonderful time she had had and got ready to go back. Debjyoti insisted on walking her home. Leaving the boys in the guest house Latika went down the road towards her house with Debjyoti.

They walked side by side resuming their conversation on their interest. Latika learnt that Debjyoti was also associated with an adventure club back in Guwahati and had trekked lots of peaks in the Himalayas. His latest being the Tawang trip in Arunachal Pradesh last winter. He promised to show her some of the pictures of the trek once they got back.

In few minutes they had reached her cottage. It was still locked. Snehlata had not returned yet. Latika opened the gates to the house and invited Debjyoti inside but he refused politely. She thanked him again for a delightful day and he disclosed that he too enjoyed the day with her. Then he finally shook hands with her and left.

Latika opened the doors of the cottage and went inside. Once all alone she slowly undressed and turned on the electric geyser in the bathroom. In few moments hot water flushed through the tap and she drenched herself under it. As the water spilled over her naked body she felt a strange sensation. Her body ached with the exertion of the day but as she closed her eyes the events of the day flashed past her eyes like a rewinding tape. She could not understand whether the excitement was of the trek or meeting Debjyoti. She kept reminding herself that it was due to her guilt that she wanted to meet him and apologize but her heart won't listen. Finally she gave up and let it wander away. It instantly relieved her.

After dressing up she prepared herself a hot cup of tea and munched on some biscuits with it. The day had been very pleasant she thought and desperately waited for her aunt to return so that she could disclose the events of the day to her. When Snehlata returned she was amazed to see her niece so happy. She wondered what had happened. Latika told her everything about her day and was excited that whatever misconception she had in her office has finally been resolved. Snehlata was happy to learn it. In fact she was glad to know that Latika was looking forward to start working again after going back.

Next day Debjyoti left for Guwahati in the morning. He called up Latika before leaving. She said that she would join next week. They stayed in Shillong for few more days then returned back to Guwahati.

Chapter Fifteen

Latika resumed her job in the office. She was informed to be assigned a new team of volunteers and a different work area. Prachi was already handling Latika's previous project and that too with perfection. So the team leader did not wanted to create any disturbances in Prachi's team. Latika did not have any problem with the new assignment. She was quite eager to start into her new venture. This time she thought of targeting the Miyan Patti which was on the other side of the Bharalu. The area was very conservative due to majority of Muslim inhabitants of Bengali origin. It was also the most neglected area in the entire slum as the community was more or less termed "Bangladeshi" openly by the locals. It was the least visited area by all the agencies. The authorities had intervened here many times to demolish it permanently but every time they turned their back on the community would sprang up once more.

Once again Latika asked for Shamsuddin's help. Over the period she had grown so accustomed to his presence during her visits to the slum that venturing out with her team in the day without a prior survey with him seemed futile to her. He was just by her side as always taking her to the other side of Bharulu this time to meet people more of his kind. He knew at heart that she would face a different scenario all together. People more poverty stricken and helpless than what she had seen in other areas. It did not take Latika a minute to judge that this part of the slum was no less than an alien world. This part of the slum was by far almost inadequate for any human inhabitation. It was in a most pathetic condition than she could imagine.

Some of the people were residing in tents made of plastic sheets by the side of drain. They cooked outside and the surrounding was filthier. Children defecated and littered nearby the tents totally unaware of its consequences. Women were mothering six to eight children at the minimum almost in all the families. Latika also found cases of teenage pregnancy and child mothers. To make the matters worse she also found the women more hostile to respond. The people in the area were tortured so much that small intervention by any outsider provoked them. They believed if no one intruded then safer they will be. The fear of losing what they least had was so strong in them that they even turned violent on slightest provocation.

Shamshuddin knew very well how it felt to be tagged as an illegal migrant. Though technically speaking he was a victim of careless administration for the tag but that did not change his situation much. He too had to bear the bruise because of the tag and was still doing. But luckily with Snehlata at his side he survived. Like him there were numerous others in the locality who were not so lucky. For them each day began with fight for survival. Leaving their families behind in far off villages they come to these big cities for livelihood and end up doing all odd jobs at half the price because of the tag. From working as a mason, laborer, rickshaw puller, roadside vegetable seller they end up doing just about anything that come their way. And if they succeed to bring in their families then the women also work with them in the construction site or if they are lucky enough then get a chance to work as a maid in some middle class homes which are not that religiously biased and that too at much less a price. However, with so much said, they are deprived of even the basic necessities of life like the ration card, bank saving account, gas connection and many more things to mention. The main enemy of such people was poverty and illiteracy, which made them alien in their own country and due to lack of proper documentation they are forced to live as an illegal migrant.

"Illegal migrant" the term itself needed a clear specification. All the Bengali speaking Muslims in the state cannot be termed as "Bangladeshi" however the toll of actual such figures is definitely a huge concern to the national security. But people like Shamsuddin also need to be addressed who are somewhere lost in between the thin line of demarcation. They have no means to prove their citizenship in India and were in many ways deprived of their basic rights. In muted lines Shaymshuddin narrated his own problem to Latika as they surveyed the locality. Latika did understand some of it but not all. Of course she had never really handled such issues in her life. For all she knew was, a Muslim was a big no-no in a Hindu house in her native place and that's about it. But she chose to break the barrier at her home and life. But apart from that she had never really come across the challenges which people like Shamsuddin faced in the state.

The morning had been an eye opener for her. She did not go to the field that day instead researched the Google for issues which Shamsuddin had narrated to her. She also had a brief discussion about it with Debjyoti and Nayanmoni in the office. Strangely their knowledge about the subject elated her. They said that Assam as a state has been facing the problem of infiltration since 1940s. But due to political intervention the problem has not come up with any solution. They said the political parties use these people as their "vote bank" to come to power. These political parties were the original culprits and very meticulously allow the "Bangladeshis" to reside in the state and legalize them by providing with voter identity card and ration card. Also cases have come up where these "Bangladeshis" easily migrate to metro cities like Mumbai and Delhi after infiltrating through the states of Assam and West Bengal. They also said that the Bodoland issue in the state of Assam was a live example of consequence of illegal infiltration from Bangladesh wherein the BODOS want a separate state and the Bengali speaking Muslims in the area were termed as "illegal migrants".

Latika was confused. She was not getting the answer. Her question was if all the Bengali speaking Muslims in the state were really "illegal migrants". To which Debjyoti denied. He said according to the government accord "People who have migrated to India on or before 1971 and their decedents are considered the citizen of India. And those after that should be termed as "illegal migrants." So far all the promises made by political parties to deport these Bangladeshis had failed for various reasons. Mostly because of political reason. Moreover these people were clever enough to change their name to Hindu names once they land in India to avoid detection or migrate to other big cities of the country.

Latika remembered such area in Delhi, Seemapuri and Geeta Colony, which were dominated by Bengali Muslim community. She wondered how the thought never crossed her mind when she resided in Delhi.

Debjyoti further highlighted Latika that even though the people can easily identify the illegal migrants in the city yet they hire these people as they are paid cheaper than the locals. This actually pulls in more migrants to the city in search of livelihood whereas the local is further deprived of job in his native place. This creates tension among the workforce that takes up nasty turn from time to time. So indeed the situation was a big threat to the future of the country.

Latika thought for a while. She memorized the scene she had come across in the morning while taking a survey with Shamsuddin. The people literally lived in pathetic condition in the locality. Health and hygiene was a Greek to them. They were nothing less than animals on the street fending for their life every day. Yet their number increased every day. The thought crossed her mind, "Were they really illegal migrants who have come all the way from a different country with a hope to have a better living?" But the realty was entirely different. What she saw there could not have been worse than in their homeland. And if it was true then why were they still infiltrating with a hope that did not exists in realty.

Debjyoti sensed her turmoil. "Whats bugging you now?" he asked pulling a chair across her.

Latika looked at him and shared her thought, "Are all the people down there illegal migrants from Bangladesh. "

"No. That's not the case always. You must first understand the term "illegal migrants". Every family residing in the locality may be Bengali Muslim but not necessarily a Bangladeshi. Let's take a peek down the history to understand this fact.

"During British Rule many families were encouraged to migrate to the low lying areas of the Brahmaputra valley from then undivided Bengal as mode of cheap labor for agriculture. They were provided land to cultivate under then zamidari system which did not allow them any ownership. Though for generations they have possessed the land yet it was never really transferred to them legally. The British and the zamindars exploited these migrants which were Muslims in majority for their benefit as the community consisted of skilled weavers, artisans and many more with skilled hands. They were looked upon as machines only meant for generating revenues for the British Empire and never shown any concern for development and welfare. They were deprived of basic education and provisions making their life miserable. Illiteracy and poverty only pushed them further to fend for means of survival than any other things. They could never think beyond food, clothes and house let alone their rights."

He continued, "Even after independence things have not changed for them. Even today the land which they reside upon or cultivate have no legal documentation and lack of which renders them as illegal occupants even after fourth or fifth generation and thus tagged as "Bangladeshi". Even after so many years they still lack the basic necessities of life and the governing bodies hardly looks into their matter. They are still fighting for survival in their own country which does not even acknowledge their existence. However, they are the ones whose skillful hands are erecting the towers in the big cities or designing the gold jewelries or weaving handlooms. You will be surprised to know that they are also known for their major contributor not just in the agricultural sector but also in poultry farming of the state of Assam. Without them egg, meat, chicken and other products would have cost the state a huge amount to import. Nevertheless they are the most victimized sector of our society today both in the hands of natural disaster or ethic calamities or the politics. And we, without any consideration, tag them as Bangladeshis."

Nayanmoni added his knowledge about the subject further. "You know Latika, I and my ancestors have lived in Assam and shall continue to live for more generations to come. Miya Muslims as the Muslims with Bengali origin are usually called have been part of our life as much as I can remember. From building our house, to selling vegetables or pulling rickshaw or as a kid I was often dropped and picked from my school by their rickshaw van. Yet till now we have never kind of accepted them as part of our main stream society no matter how well they speak our language or have accepted our culture or celebrate our festivals. For us they have always remained an outsider whereas the Assamese Muslims who are also in good number in the state have well acceptance by all the Assamese society. Comparatively they are much flourished and cultured than the Miya Muslims. The main reason lies in illiteracy and poverty which has down trodden this community completely."

"The problem started when large influx of immigration occurred after partition from then East Pakistan in 1947 and later after the consequences leading to the birth of Bangladesh. Many Hindus, to escape the atrocities of the Muslim during the Bangladesh Liberation war, had sought refuge in West Bengal and Assam causing a major crisis in the infrastructure of both the state. But the infiltration did not stop after that. It continued with majority Muslim families taking refuge illegally in the bordering areas of the state to escape poor economic situation in Bangladesh. These poverty stricken illegal migrants started affected the economy of the locals for cheap wages and thus the conflict started. The situation was worst during 1979 to 1985 wherein the state witnessed a series of agitation, riots, strikes, government instability and even emergency rule that paralyzed the whole state."

"Then finally the Assam Accord was signed in 1985 according to which those taking refuge after 25th March, 1971 are termed as "illegal migrants" and need to be deported back to their country but no steps have so far been initiated in the direction so far. During this tenure that I have just mentioned to you people both Assamese and the non-Assamese community had witnessed the bloodshed. I had lost some of my dear ones in one of these riots. So Latika you see, how badly our economic growth and opportunities are affected by these illegal migrants. It's just like a jug that will overflow once the water reaches the top. So we are actually sitting on a time bomb that can explode any minute."

"Now coming back to you question" He addressed Latika, "about the Miya Muslims. Although they have been part of our life for over five generations now yet not accepted in the mainstream of the state due to the heavy influx of Muslims from Bangladesh. Their identity was somewhere lost in the anti-Muslim agitation that burned down the entire state few decades back. Their actual figure is lost among the influx. Actually they have been so much exploited for generation in the hands of powerful communities that they hardly think beyond survival. And as Debjyoti said you can find them just about anywhere fighting for survival. They hardly know about their rights and illiterate enough to stand up for it. Their plight has succeeded generation after generation and it will continue if the government does not intervene which does not seem to happen in near future. "

Naynmoni paused to check his cell phone that was ringing. He gestured Debjyoti to take over and left the room to attend a call. Debjyoti further continued.

"Now the question is how they have reached big cities? You see our state, Assam, has a history of misfortunes, sometimes in the name of communal riots, ethnic riots or in the hands of natural calamity like flood and earthquake that has considerably affected our economic growth. So people are bound to go elsewhere for livelihood. If they have relatives in big cities they migrate there where in due course you will find a new urban slum coming up eventually."

"But, Debjyoti, the government rehabilitates the victims during these clamities isn't it?" Latika asked.

Debjyoti laughed out. "Sorry about that but what rehabilitation are you talking about? Have you visited any relief camp? The situation is pathetic. These camps are time bound and after sometime the people are left to fend on their own. Of course people continue to live there if they have no option to go else where. But the government rehabilitation programs? They are offered at eternity. So wherever these people find an opportunity they go." He paused then said, "I personally don't want you to go to work in *Miyan Patti*. Avoid it as much as you can."

Latika was speechless. She recovered shortly then asked," But why do you so so? There are many people in the area who are battling for their identity in their own country and that too without a fault of their own."

"I think there are many more areas you can cover other than that for the time." Debjyoti answered.

Latika frowned and asked, "Are we doing anything about it as an NGO when we know people there need us badly?" The question was so direct that Debjyoti paused before answering. He figured out she was very disturbed with the fact.

"Well yes. We work unbiased. Our main aim is to educate people and we believe only through proper education we can make people aware of their rights and responsibilities. You know Latika poverty is the biggest enemy of this country. These women you talked about in the locality mothering six to eight children have a pre set mind. They believe more the hands in the family means more the income. But in the run they forget that the hands need to be nurtured too. So in the battle to earn more they end up with more mouths to feed than they can possibly provide with and thus become more poor and needy. They eventually end up in the vicious circle for the rest of their life. So Latika only education can help them and make them realize their problem. And we are solely committed to that. " Debjoti paused and looked at Latika for her response.

Latika was watching him closely. "Why would you say no to me?"

"Because I want you to work in other area for now. We can think about it later."

Latika was not convinced. She knew she would go there with team or without but she didn't want to annoy Debjyoti as of now. She broke into a smile and said, "You know what Debjyoti, you made my day. I was so goddamn confused and scared since the morning that I did not know what to do but you simply enlightened me and showed me the path. THANK YOU. "

Debjoti could not believe her turn of words but he didn't pry further. He got up from the chair and bowed to her. "Always at your service mam."

They both started laughing. "You are one of a kind Latika. You made me so nervous when you stepped into my office today. I wondered what had happened. I was so bothered if I had irate you again for something but I could not think of any. Thanks to YOU mam that all is well between us or I wonder where I have to look for you this time."

Latika gave a puzzled look and said, "Look for me?"

"Well I called up your home when you didn't turn up in the office the other day. Your father told me that you have been to Shillong with your aunt."

"So we didn't meet by chance then?" Her looks didn't change.

"Well sort of you can say. But then Shillong is a big city after all and I had no clue where to find you." He paused for a while and looked at Latika. She was giving him a whimsical look.

He snapped at her with a smile, "You stop giving me that look. Seriously I didn't mean to….It was a sheer coincidence that we met. Frankly I was disturbed by your sudden disappearance." He paused and searched for her eyes again then continued, "Well I have authorities to report to about my best team member you see."

Latika smiled and said, "I hope nothing is cooking. Right?"

She poked him. He shrugged and disappeared out of the room.

Latika was left bewildered.

Chapter Sixteen

It was late in the morning but Shamsuddin was still not up yet. His back ached badly and he was having difficulty getting out of his bed. The goats were looking at him with curious eyes. The sun was already up and they were still locked up in the barn. The look in their eyes told that they wanted to get out through the barn door and into the open field grazing.

Meeeh......mehhh..........mehhhhhhhh

They called from the barn.

Usually by the time Snehlata woke up Shamsuddin would be out in the field with the goats. And by the time he returned she would be ready with her cup of hot red tea. But today she opened her eyes to the cries of her cattle. She was worried hearing them in the house. She quickly got out of her bed and ran towards the barn. The door of the barn was locked from inside.

"Shamsuddin…..Shamsuddin……." she shakily called him.

"*Ho Mami,*" Shamsuddin answered from inside.

"What happened? Are you alright?" she asked quite concerned.

"*Ho.* My back is aching very badly *Mami.* I cannot get up," he replied weakly.

"Come on man. Just try. I cannot break open the door myself," begged Snehlata from outside.

Shamsuddin did not reply. He put in all his efforts to get up and succeeded in opening the latch. But could not stand steadily and collapsed on the ground.

Snehlata ran to support him. He was sweating severely and still making efforts to reach the bed. Snehlata somehow managed to help him crawl to the bed and then supported him to get onto it.

"Just lay still. I will get help." Snehlata replied.

She called up Latika and asked her to come down immediately. Meanwhile she asked Shamsuddin about the problem. He showed Snehlata his back where it ached badly. She quickly went inside her room and returned with a painkiller spray. She applied it where Shamsuddin had showed her. In few minutes the pain killer started its action and Shamsuddin's expression changed. He looked relaxed.

"*Mami* these goats…."

"Don't worry. I will take care of them." Snehlata said and took the lot of cattle out of the barn. They followed her to the field and she left them there to graze. Over the years they were trained enough to know their route back home.

So Snehlata had nothing to worry about them. Instead her thoughts were focused on Shamsuddin's condition. For last couple of days she had seen him walk with a slight arched back. He had complained to her about mild back ache many times but she did not figure out that it could be so worse over the time.

She returned by his side after freshening up and asked if he needed anything. He shook his head and lay still with his eyes closed. After a long painful night he got relief with the painkiller. He looked up at the old lady and thanked her but she warned him that it was just temporary relief and the pain would recur once the medicine effect was over.

"You must visit a doctor anyway today. You have already delayed it so far. I have warned you many times not to neglect the pain," she said.

"I will *Mami*," he assured her and closed his eyes again.

Snehlata left him at peace and closed the door behind her. Later Latika came and Snehlata informed her about his condition.

"How is he now?" Latika asked.

"He is sleeping. I told him to visit a doctor today. If you don't mind can you go along? Your uncle is also not here otherwise I would not have troubled you." The old lady pleaded.

"Don't say that *Pishi*. Shamsuddin has helped me many times. I would love to help him out this time," said Latika.

Snehlata thanked her. Latika then fixed an appointment with the doctor and accompanied Shamsuddin to his clinic. The doctor made his investigation and asked him if he had been lifting heavy items lately. To which Shamsuddin disclosed that he had been working in a cement godown lately lifting the heavy sacks. The doctor advised him to refrain it immediately otherwise his spinal cord will be damaged permanently.

On their way back Latika bought the prescribed medicines and showed her displeasure to Shamsuddin for not disclosing his problem to her earlier wherein they met almost every other day.

Shamsuddin replied to her in a weak tone, "I am a daily laborer *Didi*. How can I afford to take rest or complain about my ill health even for a day? We are born to work every day till death. And a daily wager like me cannot decide to choose his job. He has to take whatever comes his way otherwise how he can feed his family. "

It hurt Latika to learn that but then every word he uttered was true. People like him eat only when they earn. So for them work is the first priority. But here was a man who could no longer do what he had been doing. So an alternative has to be set for him otherwise it would break him completely. She thought of helping him anyhow.

She dropped him back at her aunt's place and advised him to take complete rest for few days. She also said she would visit him whenever she had time and would know about his progress from her aunt every other day.

Shaymshuddin was overwhelmed hearing it. His eyes were moist. His family had never even inquired about him all these years since his last visit to his brother's place. The manner they had shut the door on his face was still fresh in his memory. But Allah has sent him his angels in the form of these two ladies who were not related to him in any way but were taking pain to look after him.

The ones he was destined to live with had abandoned him without giving him a second chance. Shamsuddin wept quietly as he lay on his cot in the barn. Although he knew he had made a mistake in the past but should it take so long for his kin to forgive him. They have almost wiped him off from their life. He wondered how big his son was now and whether his elder daughter was married off or not. And that his wife still loved him or not and if she did then why was she not coming back to him.

Lying on the cot helplessly Shamsuddin remembered the good times he had shared with his wife Amina. She was still a child when he had wedded her. How his mother would teach his child bride about ways to care for her husband. How she would often weep to go back to her parents place and Shamsuddin would console her saying he loved her so much that he would die if she left. And she believed him. Yes of course he had always loved Amina and she had loved him back all these years and together they parented five children. They were so much in love.

He remembered the time he had returned from Guwahati for the first time. It was Eid and Amina was looking very beautiful in the green sari with zari border he had brought for her from Guwahati. He knew she had dressed up only for him that day. Her charcoaled black eyes were always on the search for him as if they would never take the gaze off him. The green glass bangles on her hands jingled all the time as if yearning to twist around his neck and draw him closer. The faint tinkling of her anklets was disclosing the restlessness in her of having him so near after such a long time. And yet she was maintaining a decent distance from him till the night fall. The day was entirely for his children, his mother and acquaintances paying a visit their house to celebrate Eid. But as the hours passed by and the day gave way to night he too could feel the desire growing inside him. He knew his home won't be convenient enough for their meeting after such a long month of separation and thus he had made another arrangement to make the occasion special and private.

He remembered how he had borrowed a boat with a small bamboo enclosure in the middle from his friend and just before dinner had tip toed out to make the arrangements. He had brought a mattress and a blanket to make a bed. Then he randomly spread *Rajnigandha* petals on it. He placed the pocket radio that he had bought for her under the mattress. Then he went to the village shop and ordered a plate of fish fry and fish cutlet. He also picked up two *Metha patti pan* on his way back. Very carefully he tucked away everything out of sight in the boat and returned back home.

Finally the time came when all his children were asleep and his mother too had retired to her room. He had caught hold of Amina's hand and went out of the house locking the door behind. As he neared the boat he had felt his excitement grow but he held himself. Amina had stood by his side watching the Beki River and the boat ahead of them. He turned to her and whispered in her ears, "Come."

She had followed him onto the boat and it started sailing along the wind. At a considerable distance from the shore he had let down the anchors and made sure the boat was steady enough. Then he had gone to Amina who sat cautiously on the makeshift bed inside the enclosure. In the dim light of the lantern he had clubbed her face in his palms. Amina had slowly lowered her lashes in shyness. His eyes had been searching for her eyes as his hands roved all over her body.

He could still feel her soft body in his hands as he lay on his cot in the barn. He opened his eyes looking for her but was disheartened to find himself alone in the barn. He closed his eyes again and let his mind drift once more in the past. Everything flashed past his eyes as if it were happening then.

She melted in his arms hiding her face in his hairy chest. And when she finally met his gaze he could read them easily. They were screaming for him to calm her down from the fire of desire that had her burning all these days. He too could not stop himself and took her in him completely. After their blast they lay in each other's arm almost naked satisfied and happy. They had the entire night ahead of them and their privacy. So they were in no hurry. He muffled through her hair as she rested her head on his chest, her free hand feeling every part of his body. A tear rolled down the corner of her eye and on his chest.

"What happened you are crying?" He asked wiping her eyes.

"You are working so hard there and not taking care of yourself. See you have lost so much weight? "

"You are not there to take care of me you see,"

"Well then, take me with you. At least you will have me to look after you when you come back from work there."

"I am trying Amina......but you see big cities have big expenses. So I shall call you when I have enough money."

"It's very difficult to live here without you."

"Oh Amina. Even I am having difficulty living there without you people. I promise I shall take you all with me very soon."

He planted several kisses on her and gave her the little present, the pocket radio, he got for her. She was overjoyed taking it.

"Now every time you miss me turn it on and assume I am singing for you."

She giggled at her precious gift. Then they had the fish fry and *Mitha patti paan*. The ripples of the waves splashed past the wooden boat as they made love again. As the dawn was breaking they headed towards their home. It was a night that none of them could ever forget.

Tears rolled down his cheeks as he thought of the moment lying all alone in his cot in the barn among the cattle. His heart yearned for her even in his helplessness. How could she forget how much he loved her? He remembered the look in her eyes when he met him that fateful day at his brother's house. She was weeping while the bulge of her pregnancy screamed out of her betrayal. She had shamelessly admitted to stay with Fakru rather than him. Even his own son had insulted him.

"Maybe Fakru had cast a spell of black magic on them and hence they have turned against me," thought Shamsuddin.

But then he too had not fulfilled his promise to Amina. Instead of bringing them to Guwahati with him he had left them at Fakru's care like a fool. And even till date he had not succeeded in arranging for a house. The very thought that he would die without his house frightened him.

Ten years. Ten years was a long time. He was infuriated with himself. He had wasted enough time and could not waste anymore lying down on the cot vulnerably. He had to get well soon and start working. He had a house to arrange and bring in his family to Guwahati. The thoughts strengthened him and within a week he was on his feet once more.

Chapter Seventeen

As usual Shamsuddin sat on the verandah for his morning tea. Snehlata was very happy to see him fit once more. She handed him the cup of red tea and two biscuits. Together they sat, she on her kitchen stool and he on the verandah stairs, enjoying the morning along with their tea. Snehlata broke the silence.

"So you are off to work today?"

"*Ho Mami*. After almost a week. I can never repay what you and Latika *Didi* did for me."

"You have started again! You are family Shamsuddin. We have done nothing for you to brag about every time you see us. We are happy to see you well."

Shamsuddin was short of words. Of course no words can convey his thanks to them. He sipped his tea quietly.

"Just remember one thing," Snehlata continued, "Do not take any job that involves lifting heavy weight. You remember what the doctor had advised you?"

"*Ho Mami.*"

Just then Latika came by. They were both surprised to see her at this time of the morning.

"What a pleasant surprise!" Snehlata cried. "Is everything ok?"

Latika nodded her head. "I brought something for Shamsuddin," she said turning to him.

"For me?" Shamsuddin was taken aback.

Latika smiled and asked them out to the gate. They followed her silently and saw a cycle rickshaw waiting on the road. They both looked at Latika puzzled.

"What?" Latika asked as her mouth quirked. She added quickly, "This is for you, Shamsuddin."

Shamsuddin's jaw dropped hearing it. He could not believe what she just said. Meanwhile Latika continued.

"I think this will be better option for you to earn your livelihood rather than lifting sacks in the godown. It's a gift from us."

Shamsuddin broke down. He kneeled down on the road as the tears rolled down from his eyes.

"Oh *Didi.*" He sobbed like a child.

"It is a sheer surprise, Latika. I am really thankful to you that you have such consideration for Shamsuddin. God bless you my child," saying Snehlata hugged her.

"No *Pishi.* I think Shamsuddin deserves better. You have done so much for him already now it's my turn," Latika replied. She turned to Shamsuddin who was still kneeling on the ground.

"So Shamsuddin, I hope you like it."

Shamsuddin got up and thanked her again and again. He could not think of any words to say more. Both the ladies went inside the house leaving Shamsuddin outside with his new cycle rickshaw. Once alone Shamsuddin thanked The Allah for his mercy and thoughtfulness.

****

A few days later Shamsuddin visited Latika at her office and revealed his desire to offer his services for the NGO. Their project sometimes required a vehicle to carry necessary items for free distribution in the slum. Other than hand cart and cycle rickshaw other means of transportation was unable to ply on the narrow lanes of the slum colonies. So when Shamsuddin offered his services Latika informed Debjyoti and he readily agreed.

From then on he would load the materials for distribution in his rickshaw and deliver it in the specified location in the slum where the volunteers disbursed it among the needy. Other times he ferried passengers in his rickshaw nearby the market area of the Kalapahar area to earn his livelihood. Sometimes in the morning he would accompany Latika for her usual survey in the slum area in his rickshaw.

It was one such morning. Latika was heading for the tea stall near Bharalu with Shamsuddin in his rickshaw. It was pleasant morning. They left the rickshaw by the side of the road and walked to the tea stall. The old man greeted them with a smile. Over the time she was a regular visitor to his tea stall. She conducted her team meetings with her volunteers almost every day there over a cup of tea. Then they would disperse in different lanes in the colonies and finally met again in the evening before returning to the office.

Latika took her seat in one of the wooden benches lying outside the stall and ordered for two cup of tea. The old man started preparing tea and asked her if she was still looking for the Muslim women she had mentioned him once.

"Did you come across her, *Baba*?" Latika asked quite amazed. It had been almost seven months now that she had enquired him about the woman.

"I think so." He replied as he stirred a spoon in his tea saucepan.

"How do you know it was her?" she asked.

"Actually she came looking for some volunteers from the NGO. I told her that you visit here with your team in the day. She even waited for sometime but then left. She was looking very worried. I asked her about the problem but she did not answer." He replied.

"Did she tell you where she lived?" Latika was concerned.

"No. She didn't. But she was a Bengali Muslim woman. So most probably she must be living somewhere in the other side of the Bharalu. Their community people mostly reside in that part of the basti." He answered.

Latika was worried. Over months her priority of searching the Muslim woman had taken the back seat due to her sociall work. Alhough she always wanted to work in the other side of the Bharalu but her work limitations forbidded her. The information was a major breakthrough and she had a reason to go there. But she knew she would defy Debjyoti's instruction.

She thanked the old man for the information and finished her tea quickly. She decided to go to the *Miyan*

Patti in search of the woman. Of course she had nothing to worry as long as Shamsuddin accompanied her. He agreed to go with her without any second thought. Together they crossed the narrow bamboo bridge over the Bharalu River and reached the locality.

Although Latika knew she would be looking for a needle in the hay she thought of giving it a try. She still remembered the woman and the girl who visited the health camp that day. So even if she did not succeed she would at least be happy that she tried. They roamed about the lanes along the cluster of houses bustling with people. She moved aimlessly from one lane to the other but her eyes were on the search. She didn't care about the people who were eyeing her out of curiosity and enmity. She knew they disliked her very presence here yet she moved on.

Finally she reached the place where the women of the locality came to fetch drinking water. She could not help wincing. It was an open well with pool of stinking stagnant water surrounding it almost contaminating the drinking water. Different slabs of stones on the pool of water lead to the opening of the well where the ladies filled their water pitcher.

The very sight screamed of various diseases the people here were prone to after drinking this water. Latika covered her nose with her dupatta and looked around. She was quite sure that someone around could give her a clue about the woman she was searching for. Shamsuddin was standing a few meters away from her at the back.

She was still looking for someone to speak to when she heard Shamsuddin scream. As she turned back, something hit her hard in the head. She lost her balance and toppled in the pool of water while her head stuck the stone slab with a thud. Blood oozed out from her temple and blended slowly with the dirty water of the pool. The impact was so hard that she blacked out instantly.

Shamsuddin came charging towards the man who had smack Latika but he was no match for the heavysized man. Next second he too was licking the dust from the ground. The man did not make any advances instead warned Shamsuddin of dire consequences if they made further intrusion in the colony and left leaving the two wounded to fend for themselves on the ground. Shamsuddin shouted for help. He was screaming and calling names to the people who had gathered around to see in his mother tongue which they too spoke and understood.

"You son of bitches! You will never get better. See you have killed the light of hope yourself. This woman was here to help you. I am no different than you but you chose to rot in hell. Allah had sent this angel to you but see what you did to her. He will punish you now. You scoundrels….how dare…."

He kept shouting at them while blood dripped from his forehead and nose drenching his shirt but he did not care. He was furious but the people showed no response. It was a common sight for them as people brawled almost everyday over drinking water here. They showed neither remorse nor any sign of help while Shamsuddin kept shouting.

Latika lay motionless in the pool of water bleeding. All of a sudden a lady appeared from among the crowd and ran to help Latika. She lifted Latika's head in her lap and wrapped a cloth around the wound to stop the bleeding. Then she called Shamsuddin who was still calling names to the people. In his anger he had completely forgotten about Latika. He got up and ran towards Latika. He lifted her in his arms with the lady's help and walked fast towards his rickshaw parked at the other side of the Bharalu. The lady walked beside them still holding the piece of cloth around Latika's wound. Somehow they managed to reach the nearest clinic.

Chapter Eighteen

Latika opened her eyes slowly. The room looked unfamiliar to her. She tried to open both her eyes but her right eye did not open beyond what it already did. She lifted her hand to it slowly and felt the bulge in her right eye which was restricting the eye lid to open further. She further caressed her forehead which was bandaged and ached a little.

"Stay still." A voice instructed her.

She moved her eyes towards the source. A man in white apron stood at the other end of her bed examining her reports. Latika realized she was in a hospital.

"Doctor! How bad is it?" she asked the man scrutinizing her reports.

"Not that bad. It is a case of acute subdural hematoma, blood clotting in brain, which means you will be under observation for few days before you are released from the hospital," replied the doctor.

"Is that serious?" She said trying to get up.

"No, But we will make sure everything is fine before we let you go. So don't panic at all! You are just about fine and around a week's time fit to go home. OK?" He assured her.

Latika nodded.

"So let me send your folks in. They have been waiting outside to see you." The doctor said moving out.

Snehlata and her father walked in the tiny hospital room. The look on their face told her how worried thay have been for her all the while. Snehlata sat by her side and caressed her while her father clenched her hand. It was pity to see them both so troubled she thought and smiled at them to assure that everything was fine. They talked for few minutes as the doctor did not allow them much time to visit. Her father was eyeing her with pitiful eyes as she talked to her aunt. Then before going out he patted her cheeks lovingly and then left the room closing the door behind.

Latika lay in the bed thinking. She remembered she was hit by a man and then she blacked out. She wondered how she had reached the hospital and what happened to Shamsuddin. It did not take her much time to get her answer. Her colleagues, Prachi and Sachin, come to visit her shortly afterwards. They were in shock to see her swollen eye and bandaged head but didn't express. Instead they gave a big smile and wished for her fast recovery. They told her that it was Shamsuddin who had brought her to a clinic.

Latika was overwhelmed by Shamsuddin's gesture. She knew very well how difficult it might have been for him to get her any medical assistance nearby the slum and wanted to thank him. But he had not visited her yet.

Prachi and Sachin left after spending some time with her. Latika eagerly looked at the closed door with her half open eye for someone to come by. But the door only opened for nurses and doctor who came to check her out on routine basis. The day gave way to evening. But no visitor came except for her father and Snehlata. They spent some time with her and then proceeded to check for her improvement from the doctor.

When Latika came to know that her father had been up the whole night the night before in the hospital she clearly denied them to stay the following night. She assured them that she will be fine through the night and they can meet her next morning. They were little sceptical but when the doctor said that there was nothing to worry they both agreed and went back home.

****

Latika lay still in her hospital bed thinking of the long night ahead. She longed for somebody to drop by. She wanted to talk but apart from nurses nobody came. She tried to sit down but could not. She lay quietly in her bed. She thought of her father. The old man was so much in distress to find his daughter in this condition. There was nobody to look after him at home. She felt very low thinking about it.

Eventually her thoughts drifted to her office. She recalled the look in Prachi and Sachin's eyes that they were terrified to death looking at her condition. "Did I look so bad?" she asked herself. She wanted to ask for a mirror from the nurse to see herself but dropped the idea as her reflection might haunt her for days to come.

She thought of Debjyoti and Nayanmoni. She remembered Nayanmoni had been to Delhi for some meeting. But Debjyoti was in town and it annoyed her that he had not come to visit her in the hospital. After all he was the boss and it was his duty. But she was startled to find that her anger was more targeted towards the relationship she had developed for him. After their short encounter at Shillong he was more of a friend to her than her team leader. Although they did not get to interact much like they had in Shillong but their gesture and body language had changed to informal lately. She frowned at the thought and diverted her mind to lesser important topic.

Shortly her dinner was served which she finished with little disapproval. She wondered how long it would be before she could get the taste of her favorite fish curry. She tried to get some sleep. As she closed her eyes sleep drifted her without any intimation and started dreaming. The incident of the previous morning flashed up in front of her eyes like a bullet. She remembered Shamsuddin's shriek and then her fall on the stone slab. It was so painful that she screamed in her dream and tried to jerk out of the bed. Someone was holding her. She opened her eyes and saw Debjyoti calming her down.

She could not understand anything first. Then the surrounding of the room invoked her senses. She looked straight into his eyes. He was standing just by her side near the bed, his hands still holding her hand and patting gently. She withdrew her hand instantly and tried to sit up.

"No don't. Your head will ache," he said gently pushing her back.

"What are you doing here at this hour?" she asked without any hesitation.

Debjyoti looked for something to sit down. He found a stool and pulled it near her bed. He sat down comfortably and replied in an easy going tone.

"Babysitting you."

She looked back at him. Annoyed. The feeling without any intimation engulfed her. She didn't know the reason. But she was furious at something or someone.

"I didn't ask for it. I am fine. You can leave now." She sounded angry.

His eyes were sad as he looked down at her. She looked exactly out of a horror flick with her smashed head and bulging eye. But that did not bother him. What concerned him was the pain she was going through.

He replied calmly, "I don't wait for instructions. I do what is the need of the hour. At this moment you need me to take care of you while you sleep."

She didn't say anything and looked away.

****

Debjyoti recalled the moment of the previous morning. His hands and feet turned cold when took the call and found Shaymshuddin on the other side of Latika's cell phone. Alarm bells had already started ringing in his mind when he had heard Shamsuddin's voice. His worst fears were coming true. Shamsuddin asked him to come immediately to the clinic.

He had not wasted a second to reach there. What he saw in the clinic was even worst. Latika's clothes were all soaked in her blood and it had even stained Shamsuddin's shirt when he had lifted her in his arms. Debjyoti did not reconsider his decision of taking her to the trauma center immediately where he knew she would be in better hands. The doctors attended to her wounds and thoroughly examined her for any serious problem.

It had been a terrible moment for both him and Shamsuddin waiting outside the emergency ward for the doctor. Shamsuddin then had told him elaborately about the whole incident. Her feisty nature had revoked her from heeding to his advices. He blamed himself for not being stricter with her from the beginning but deep down he knew why. Somehow she had managed to pry deep down his heart where he had not let anyone for so long and he hated it. He knew better that sooner or later he would give way to her demands both professionally and personally. No matter how hard he tried to tackle her situation listening to his brain but his heart would take the priority automatically.

Standing alone outside the emergency ward pacing up and down the corridor could have easily been substituted by calling up her kin and the office colleagues. Together they all would have shared the tension. But he had not informed anyone about her accident. Whatever was happening inside the emergency ward that morning was a repetition of circumstances in his life couple of years back. It seemed like he was reliving that moment of his life.

Beads of perspiration appeared on his forehead as he waited panicky for the doctor to come out. And when the doctor finally did Debjyoti just could not move. His feet were frozen up and his heart raced as if it would ogle out into his palm. He could barely listen to what the doctor was saying. Only one word caught his attention "....is fine" that brought him back to reality. He looked around and saw Shamsuddin smiling at him.

The doctor had said nothing was critical apart from a small blood clot in the brain which they had diagnosed but he could not comment till was she fully conscious. He further said she was gaining consciousness off and on. And they will keep her under observation. Otherwise she was doing fine so far.

It was such a relief to hear the doctor. Later on when Latika was shifted to a private room in the ward Debjyoti saw her for the first time. Even in unconscious state with all the bandages she looked aggressive enough fighting the battle within. But he was happy to see her fine. He then called up office and asked Sachin to take care of the office. Later he called up Latika's father and informed him about Latika saying it was a small road accident. To avoid panicking the old man furher he deliberately evaded mentioning that she was hit by a man in the slum. And when the old man came down to meet his daughter in the hospital Debjyoti stood by his side all the time to lend his support.

Later Snehlata too came to see Latika. She sat quietly by her brother's side the whole day. As the hours passed by and day give in to night Debjyoti insisted them to go home and take rest. He succeeded in sending Snehlata home but Latika's father won't listen. He insisted on staying till she recovered. Debjyoti found it awkward to leave him in the hospital alone. So after seeing off Snehlata he returned and sat in the waiting room outside the ward beside the old man.

They took turns to check upon Latika that night. Once in a while the old man broke down and Debjyoti consoled him. The old man talked about his daughter and her rebellious nature that created many problems in her life. Debjyoti patiently heard him without giving any input. He too had seen her fiery side but he did not find it appropriate to comment at this moment. He let the old man do the talking. Later in the first hour of dawn Latika regained conciousness. The doctor and his team conducted certain investigation. Later they informed Debjyoti that she was fine. Snehlata came to relieve them early morning and the duo finally left for home for some rest.

Before going home Debjyoti went to the police station and lodged a complaint though he knew nothing would be done about it. Later he called up Sachin and told him about Latika. Sachin promised to take care of everything in the office. Done with all his responsibilities Debjyoti finally hit his pillow and slept through the entire day before waking up in the evening. Later when he came back to the hospital to check upon Latika he learnt that nobody was there to attend her at night. So he decided to stay back.

Chapter Nineteen

Now sitting beside her bed he watched Latika for the first time after she regained conciousness. She looked better than the previous night but seemed upset about something. He didn't want to upset her further and sat quietly beside her bed waiting for her to go to sleep once more but Latika lay wide awake. Just to reassure her he gently took her hand in his and caressed it as if singing a lullaby to put her back to sleep.

But Latika was in no mood for that. She was terrified by her dream and Debjyoti's presence confused her. She withdrew her hand from his and looked into his eyes.

Debjyoti said without waiting for a question from her. "Try to get some sleep, Latika. You will be fine soon."

But Latika did not respond. She continued looking at him with quizzical eyes.

He was wondering what to say next. She seemed so troubled.

"Should I get you something?" he asked. Still there was no response.

"I shall call the nurse?" saying he got up to leave the room.

"No, its fine," said Latika. "I am ok. It's just the nightmare...."

"Don't worry. I am here. Now try to get some sleep." He once again sat down on the stool beside her.

"It's fine. You can leave. It's already late," Latika said.

"I can't leave you unattended throughout the night. I am staying here till morning. So don't worry. Just sleep." He urged.

She looked at him with curiosity saying, "You don't have to do that."

"Oh really! Who will calm you down if you freak out in the later part of night?" asked Debjyoti cynically. "And moreover I am used to staying awake all night."

"Your presence is confusing me." She complained.

"Why? What have I done now?" he asked puzzled.

"You have the tendency to show up when least expected." She answered quite amused.

"Don't say you didn't expect me." He chuckled. "But I cannot be your savior in the slum where you have the tendency to defy me for some reasons better known to you."

"Defy you? When did I defy you?" Latika asked.

"Why! Didn't I warn you not to venture alone in the slum and that too in Miyan Patti? And what is the point of surveying the area first," he argued. "You are good in inviting trouble and we suffer."

"I tried to help somebody and got punched." She snapped. "So it's my fault. What if...."

Debjyoti silenced her by putting his hands on her mouth. "You will never venture alone in the slum without my knowledge. Promise me." He commanded. "I can't keep telling lies to your father."

"*Bapi*? What did you say to him?"

"I told him you met with an accident. If he knows the truth then only God knows what will happen to him. He was worried to death last night praying for you. So please promise me that you will never do this again." He urged.

His statement surprised her. "You were here last night?" she asked.

"Of course I was here. You are my responsibility. " He answered without any doubt.

"What responsibility?" she asked trying to get up.

He got up to fix a pillow behind her back so that she could raise her head a little. Latika waited for his answer. She searched for his eyes but he did not meet her gaze.

"You are my teammate and I think that's enough to answer your question." He answered without any hesitation.

The answer did not satisfy Latika. She was astonished that she wanted to hear something more from him. His very presence in the room had aroused a different feeling within her which she was unable to understand. She had sensed this feeling earlier too when they had met in Shillong. As if meeting him in a different setup other than the office triggered some kind of feelings in her that seemed to nullify the void that had developed within her over the years. Even though he had plainly admitted to her about his sole reason to be in the room beside her at this hour yet it didn't please her.

She rested her head against the raised pillow and closed her eyes. She feared that if he looked down in her eyes at the moment he could easily read her thoughts and she didn't want that. In fact she did not want anybody to know her feelings.

So far she led life on her terms. Her share of both happiness and grief were entirely the consequences of her decision and she did not like anybody to intrude. Not even her parents even though they supported her every time. But they never saw her vulnerable side. The barrier she had created around her one could only see her aggressive and vibrant side. Her bruised side was well hidden from everybody. She lay quietly with her eyes closed fighting the turmoil within.

Looking at her Debjyoti thought she wanted to rest. He quietly left the room without saying any word. Latika heard his retreating footsteps but did not utter any word.

****

Next morning doctor examined her and decided to discharge her later in the evening. But she was advised to come for regular checkup for about a week. Latika's father was very happy to hear that. Snehlata insisted that they spend some days in her house till Latika was completely well. It was a good idea Latika's father thought as he was not very sure of taking good care of Latika by himself. They went to Snehlata's house from the hospital in the evening.

At Snehlata's house Latika was given a small room at the rear of the house. She lay down on the bed and looked through the window above. She saw Shamsuddin sitting in the verandah outside the kitchen. Latika drew the curtain aside and called him. He came up to window and stood on the other side of the open window panes.

"How are you *Didi*? I had been to see you twice in the hospital but you were taking rest. So I did not disturb you," he said still smiling.

"I was looking for you to thank you, Shamsuddin. Without you I wouldn't have make it that day."

"No Didi. I should not have taken you there. These people are not worth your services," he snapped. "Nobody came forward to help me except an woman, you know. These people deserve nothing better. Let them rot in hell." He was infuriated thinking of that day. Later he also told her about Debjyoti's role in the entire episode and that made Latika little sorry as she hadn't thanked him for all the touble he had taken for her.

Slowly she diverted her thoughts from him on her new surroundings. She had been to her *Pishi*'s house many times earlier when the house was full of her cousins. She remembered how they use to have blast during the summer vacation when she came down to visit her parents. But now the house bore a worn out look just like her father and aunt. How lonely the house felt without all its occupants. She was glad that Debjyoti had not disclosed about her incident to her father otherwise he would have been lying sick beside her by now. She decided to spend more time with her father from then on. Later her aunt brought her dinner which she had to her fill and went off to sleep. She had a peaceful night with no more nightmares to haunt her.

Next morning the day started very early. She moved the curtain aside and saw Shamsuddin walking the goats to the field. Her aunt's amazing liking for goats as domestic milching animals intrigued her. Later in the day she asked about it to her aunt and Snehlata disclosed her secret with pride.

"These animals were my only asset when we came down to live here," said the old lady. "We were not that well off then and these cattle were almost maintainence free. Moreover its milk is medicine for asthma."

Since then the cattle generation remained a priceless possession for her and were very much part of life. Even after so many years she cannot think of separating herself from these animals under any circumstance. They shall live in this house as long as she is alive.

Latika was happy to learn the sentiments of her aunt. The old lady although had never taken any formal education yet her practical knowledge and broad mindedness was incomparable with anyone in the family. She had put up a brave fight with her relatives and community for letting a Muslim fellow stay within her house premises. It surely takes lot of courage to take such a decision and stick by it no matter what. And Shamsuddin had spent ten years in her house. Her aunt had come a long way from her attachment with the past to the foresightedness of a modern society where people are not bracketed by their religion and caste. Latika filled up with pride for her aunt.

Latika also came to know about Shamsuddin's dream of owning a house for which he had been saving money with Snehlata. He told her about his family and how he ended up in Guwahati. However, he was clever enough to hide the fact about his family abandoning him and about his illicit affair with Geeta because of whom the entire episode started.

Meanwhile her regular visit to the doctor continued. She was gradually recovering as her headache had subsided permanently with the blood clot and she could move about freely within the house. It was a family time for her when in the evenings she would go to the temple with her aunt and played cards with her father. She would help her aunt in the kitchen sometimes and heard stories from Shamsuddin about his village. After about a week her doctor informed her that her wound had healed and she was fit now. Latika called up her office and informed them about her improvement and desire to join work. They were glad to hear about it.

Chapter Twenty

Latika joined the office the following week. Nayanmoni welcomed her with the rest of the team. She learnt that Debjyoti was out of town on some official work. Her profile took a U-turn after she rejoined the office. She was restricted from going to the field till further instruction from her team leader. Nayanmoni assigned her admin work which she did without much interest.

Nayanmoni told her about the police complaint that was filed by Debjyoti on her behalf. He told her that she had to visit the police station whenever required. Latika didn't show much interest in the case. She knew there is nothing much the police can do about it but nevertheless she thanked Nayanmoni for the information.

She also learnt that Nayanmoni had been doing a regular follow up in the case. She wondered why she had not been summoned for her statement yet. He told her Shamsuddin's statement has been recorded as the prime witness while they will contact her soon.

"Why nobody bothered to inform me about all this?" Latika argued. "I don't want any police action in the case. It has to be withdrawn."

"But Latika it is for your safety," replied Nayanmoni trying to persuade her.

"No Nayan. It will only bridge the gap further between us and them. I don't know what prompted that man to attack me that day but the fact is people there seek our help. And moreover a lady had helped us that day. With this police action whatever little faith they have in us will be washed away. I don't want this to happen. The complaint has to be withdrawn," she urged.

Nayan replied, "See Latika, I see your point. But Debjyoti is the team leader and he has the responsibility for the whole team. If he has taken a decision in this regard he must have thought about it thoroughly. I cannot defy in this matter."

"Well then I shall go to the police station and withdraw the case myself."

"You cannot do that either as the case is registered in his name. So its better we wait till he returns. Till then do as he has expected you to. I shall accompany you wherever you need me." Nayanmoni assured her.

Latika went back to her workstation. She knew Nayanmoni will be of no help to her regarding the case. Hence she did not exaggerate further. She quietly resumed the job Nayanmoni had assigned. But her brain was looking for an alternative to escape the situation.

She did not have to wait long. There was a call from the police station in the office and Nayanmoni told her to go. He too went along with her. The in-charge of the police station asked her to give the statement about the incident which she did reluctantly. But it was not of much help as she had not seen her assailant.

She learnt that the miscreants had political patronage. The incharge in muted lines advised her to take further precaution and not venture alone much. They showed her some of the photographs of the suspects from their record file to identify but Latika plainly denied them ruffling through the file pages.

Nayanmoni witnessed the whole episode sitting next to her in the police station. He could make out easily that she was not actively participating and it alarmed him for further mishaps in near future. His legs twitched a little with the thought of it as they had several volunteers working in the area.

After returning to the office he called up Debjyoti and informed him about the whole scenario. Debjyoti instructed him to ignore her pleas and refrain from going to the field under any circumstance for the time being. Nayanmoni knew he had a big job ahead till the team leader returned. But he knew it would be tougher for him to persuade Latika to sit back in the office and continue the support job.

The following few days, much to her dislike Latika worked in the office. She cheered up the volunteers every morning as they followed their team lead to the slum while she sat back taking their calls for any support or doing other admin work as notified by Nayanmoni. It had been a difficult week for her but she did not have much choice apart from doing what has been assigned to her.

Her morning survey with Shamsuddin had also stopped during this period as her father wanted her to go for walks with him. She could not deny him as it was the first time over the years he had asked to accompany him during his walks. He said he wanted to spend time with her. And after joining office this was the only suitable time which she could spend with him.

Eventually walks to the slum had been postponed for indefinite period. She knew well that none of her team members would venture into her assigned area which meant for the time being nobody visited that part of the slum. Sometimes sitting in the office Latika wondered about the woman who was looking for her in the tea stall. She prayed for the woman's well being from the core of her heart. Her prayers were answered eventually.

One morning Shamsuddin walked into her office along with a young woman. She was dusky, thin and tall woman in her early twenties. Latika learnt that she was the same lady who had helped her when she was attacked the other day. Shamsuddin told her that the woman had approached him the previous evening when he was returning after ferrying a passenger from Kumarpara. He said that the woman had recognized him and was asking about Latika.

Latika looked at the woman who sat in a chair at the corner of the room surveying the office surroundings. Latika walked up to her and thanked her for what she had done that day. But the woman said that she was the one who needed help. She asked Latika to accompany her to her house in Miyan Patti. Latika knew she could not take the call on her own. So she called Nayanmoni and told him the entire story.

"*Ho bidoh*! I am the in-charge here. You can tell me your problem," Nayanmoni told to the woman.

But the woman insisted that she would only tell Latika and for that Latika has to go with her. Nayanmoni faced the music now. He could allow Latika due to the restriction imposed and then the lady had come in for help. He was in turmoil. He went back in his cabin and tried to balance the situation. Latika followed shortly.

"What do I do now?" Nayanmoni asked Latika. "I cannot let you go there nor can I let the woman go unattended." He thought for a while then said, "Can't we ask her tomorrow?"

"She has been looking for me all the while. We don't know the problem yet. Maybe it is serious. We cannot postpone," replied Latika thoughtfully.

Nayanmoni knew she was right. "But she stays in *Miyan Patti* and I cannot allow you to go there. Ask her to come tomorrow. I shall send Prachi with her. "

Latika didn't make any move to take that excuse from him. She stood there rigidly looking at him as if asking him to reconsider his decision.

"Don't give me that look. I can't."

She pulled a chair across the table and sat comfortably before replying, "Yes sir you can. Send me off the records and any consequence shall be my responsibility."

"What are you talking about?" Nayanmoni insisted. "Are you out of your mind? Just ask her to come tomorrow or tell her I shall go right away."

"Nayan the lady has shown her trust in only me otherwise she wouldn't have been looking for me all these days out in the slum where almost all the others are working in every second lane. Just think about it. Even if you go or send somebody else tomorrow the lady might not be comfortable opening up. So let me go and Shamsuddin shall be with me. You can cover me if you want to. "

Nayanmoni thought it over then replied, "Maybe you are right. I don't know what will happen but let's go. Let me divert the calls to my cell phone while we are gone."

****

Nayanmoni and Latika followed the woman along with Shamsuddin across the wooden bridge on the other side of the Bharalu. The woman led them to the far interior of the colony. They stopped in front of a small house with mud walls not very far from the place where Latika was assaulted. The woman went inside first and returned shortly to call them in. Nayanmoni asked Shamsuddin to wait outside while they went inside.

The house was neat and clean. The lady offered them a mat on the floor to sit while she stood by the bamboo partition that separated the the other room of the house. Nayanmoni looked up at her to seek the answers that had been boggling his mind all the while. The woman narrated her story without delay.

She said her name was Nafisa and she lived with her mason husband and two sons. She looked at Latika and said that it was her sister-in-law who had visited their last health camp with her elder daughter. Latika nodded her head without interrupting.

Nafisa continued that the girl went missing few months back. They looked for the girl everywhere but refrained from lodging police complaint due to harassment. Then one day she returned all bruised and tortured. She was in shock to divulge anything about her plight and later we came to know that she was pregnant. We were still living with it when few days back the younger daughter went missing on her way to relief herself in the wee hours of the morning. Nafisa wiped off tears rolling down from her eyes.

"She is only twelve, *Bidoh*," Nafisa said looking at Latika. "I cannot even imagine her plight. We are very poor people, *Bidoh*. Please save her. We have all our hopes on you," she begged.

Both Nayanmoni and Latika were speechless hearing the lady. No words could soothe the pain the family was going through.

"We will help you in all possible ways, *Bidoh*," Nayanmoni assured the lady. "Is it possible for us to meet the girl?"

"*Ho, Dada*." The woman went inside and reappeared. She asked Latika to come in the other room. Latika followed and saw a skinny girl sitting on a stool in the room. Her bulging belly disclosed her advanced pregnancy. The girl's health had detoriated considerably over the months but Latika recognized her immediately. The girl met her gaze with moist eyes. Latika could not stop herself any longer and hugged the girl. Those eyes had been haunting her almost every night all these months and she could never forgive herself for reaching so late for help.

"Don't you worry? Now, we will take care of you," she whispered in the girl's ear.

The girl nodded her head. Later, she narrated her story to Latika. She said that she had eloped with one of her neighbour's relative, who happens to visit often, on pretext of marriage. He had told her that he worked with a big company in Delhi but once they reached there, he took her to one of his friends's house where she was confined forcefully along with two more Napalese girls. Later she came to know that the guy had sold her off to the man. For days they were physically abused and mentally tortured to give in to his demands. Then one day few more men walked in and picked up one of the Nepali girls. That day the girl realized that she has to escape to survive. Next time a cop came by and they thought he had come to rescue them but he raped them. It continued for next few days with different men walking in different times of the day. Meanwhile the other Nepalease girl had fallen real sick and was taken to hospiltal. That was the chance when she escaped from the house and returned home. She had no idea how she managed to reach Guwahati.

On reaching home she had thought her family would support her but she was wrong. They accused her and held her responsible for all the miseries she had been through. For months she lived with her stigma without any help from anybody in the family. But when her younger sister disappeared under mysterious circumstances she could not stop herself anymore. She feared her sister would also face the same fate as hers and hence stood up to fight. Her parents still did not support her. It was only her aunt, Nafisa, who understood her and promised to bring help.

"*Bidoh*, Please save my sister," sobbed the girl.

Latika nodded and moved out of the room. She looked at Nayanmoni who had overheard the conversation in the other room. Latika sat down beside him once more on the mat. She could not stop herself from asking Nafisa, "When you know about the guy why didn't you question him?"

"How can we, Bidoh? His brother-in-law has political patronage and if we even think of pointing a finger at the family we are as good as dead. We are too poor and helpless to take any action."

Nayanmoni said, "You see this is a serious offence and the culprit needs to be behind bars. You have to bring the girl to lodge a report in the police station. Are you ready?"

She looked behind in the other room. The girl replied, "No police. I cannot go to them. I will do everything to save my sister but no police. I shall not go to them." She cried.

Nafisa looked at Nayanmoni and said, "*Dada*! I don't know how to get her ready for it but still I shall try. But please tell me you will help us getting back the girl. I have lots of hope on you people. We are very poor people and nobody cares of us…we… " she was literally begging while tears were rolling down her cheeks.

Nayanmoni stood up and bowed to her folding both his hands. "We shall do everything to save your little daughter, *Bidoh*. Please don't weep like that." They came out of the house.

Chapter Twenty One

Latika saw Nayanmoni sitting in his cabin very tensed. He was looking at the fan that was revolving in full swing. His face expressionless and his eyes blank. He didn't hear her come and was startled by her question.

"What do we do now?" Latika asked sitting across the table.

There was no reply. Latika looked up at him. He was chewing the butt of a pencil thinking hard.

"We need to report the case to the police anyhow otherwise we will not be able to do anything," he replied after some time.

"But the girl has denied going to them." Latika added.

"This is lies the problem. We have to get her ready for her statement otherwise its no use. I can handle the case but not without her legal testimony." He answered.

"Maybe we should approach them again and make them understand the importance of it." Latika urged.

"The girl is terrified Latika and so is the family. We might lose their trust on us if we insist much," he replied.

"So what option we have now?" she said.

Nayanmoni looked up at her and said, "I am falling blank thinking of it. Of course it is our priority to help them but how I don't know yet. "

"What if I go and persuade the girl?" Latika suggested. "I was attacked in their locality so in a way they will sympathies with me as a victim like themselves. Maybe we get a chance there. What do you say? "

"What are you saying Latika? How can you even think of going there again and that too for this issue? They might kill you this time if they come to know that you are registering a criminal case against them. No. I cannot allow that. And moreover it is the TL's strict instruction not to let you in the field. I cannot make a decision in his absence," snapped Nayanmoni.

"I know that. But Debjyoti will return after ten days or so. Imagine what can happen by then. We must not forget a girl's life is at stake. You have to make a decision now itself," Latika urged.

In a way she was right Nayanmoni thought but he didn't have the courage to say yes to her. He kept mum and retaliated to his state of blank expression. Latika went out of the cabin fuming. Later she saw him dialing a number from the phone book. He spoke to the person on the other end for about half an hour then hung off and started jotting down something in his notebook. She did not see him come out of the cabin before evening.

That day passed off without any further discussion on the issue. Later Latika left for her home. She thought of the case throughout the time in her house. Every time the solution ended up with her going to the slum and meeting the girl. She was damn confident that she could succeed in taking the girl and her family in her confidence. She thought of calling Debjyoti. He was the one who could save the girl now she thought. The bell rang twice and there was no response. She called again but Debjyoti didn't pick up the call. She thought of leaving a message for him but didn't.

Next morning she went with her father for walk without much eagerness. Her father felt her uneasiness. "Is something bothering you dear?" He asked as they walked towards the park.

"Nothing *Bapi* just the office stuff," she replied.

"You must not let anything bother you so much dear. Many times solution lies in front of us and we are unable to seek it. So share your worries and don't let it worry you," advised the old man.

"You are right *Bapi* but sometimes our fears restraints us from doing that we yearn to do," said Latika.

"Fear is only a state of mind. So if you succeed in changing your prospective you will not be afraid anymore and can always do what you want to do," her father replied.

The words strengthened her thoughts. She pressed her father's arm in assurance and quickly matched with his pace.

****

She got ready for her office and thought gladly about the challenge of winning Nayanmoni's confidence for letting her meet the girl. She knew it would be tough but not impossible. She was charged up for that. She set out for the office with a new excitement in her. Throughout the way she was thinking of words to put across him which could change his way of thinking in some way or the other. By the time she reached her office she was quite satisfied with her preparation.

But her excitement reached the nadir when she saw Debjyoti back in the office. He was standing with his back to the entrance door and speaking with the volunteers acknowledging their progress in their respective projects. He did not see Latika walk into the office. She tip toed to her workstation without his knowledge and sat in a manner to hid herself behind the computer monitor. She needed some time to rephrase her preparation. She had no clue that Debjyoti would be here and ruin everything for her. She disliked his presence in the office at that moment. She knew quite well that with his presence it would be impossible for her to make Nyanmoni agree to her terms. She sighed with frustration thinking about it.

Eventually the volunteers left with their respective project heads. A little later Nayanmoni came to her and informed that he and Debjyoti would be out too for some work. They left after sometime and Latika sat alone in the office. For some time she fumbled thru the pages in the file that needed to be updated. But her mind was at unrest. She felt like screaming out and call names but stopped herself. She walked to the pantry and made herself a cup of red tea.

She sat down in the hall to enjoy her tea. The hot beverage running down her food pipe calmed her down. The morning paper lying on the table caught her attention. She flipped through its pages. A column on weather forecast interested her. It predicted the arrival of monsoons in few days which meant relief from the scorching summer. But the column also highlighted the possibility of flood in some areas of the state. It was nothing new though as the state of Assam witnessed flood almost every year and that too twice or thrice, once during the onset of monsoons and another during its withdrawal. Nevertheless she was glad though that the monsoon was due.

She finished her tea and returned back to her work. Time went by and it was post lunch but still there was no sign of Debjyoti and Nayanmoni. She finished her work and some more pending work that was due. Later the volunteers started returning. Prachi and Sachin also came back with their team but still the duo had not returned. Latika although stood with them but her mind was wondering elsewhere.

It was half past seven in the evening and only Prachi, Sachin and Latika were in the office. The volunteers had left for the day. Sachin asked Latika about Nayanmoni and Debjyoti. She told them that they had left in the morning.

"But they never did this before. Is anything serious?" Sachin asked.

Latika shook her head.

"Lets wait for some more time then we will make a call." Sachin suggested. "But Latika you must have some idea about what they are up to."

Latika told them about the incident.

"Oh! I see. Maybe they are trying to help the girl in some way." Sachin remarked.

Just then the phone on the table rang and Prachi took the call. Nayanmoni was on the other end. He asked for

Sachin. Sachin took the receiver from her and answered. The call went on for fifteen minutes. Then he hung up.

"What is it?" Prachi asked.

"Well, they said they will be out of station for few days and we have to take care of everything here. I have to be in the office till they return, so Prachi you alone have to address the volunteers tomorrow. "

"That's O.K. But did they say anything about where or what they are doing?" asked Prachi.

"No. They said will brief us once they are back. So I think it's already late and we can make our plans for tomorrow early in the morning. What do you say?"

"Fine. Let's call it a day then." Prachi answered.

They headed home locking the office.

Chapter Twenty Two

The office keys were with Latika so she was the first one to turn up in the office. As she opened the door the office phone started ringing. Latika ran down the hall way to pick the call. It was from their Head Office. The lady on the other end asked about the in-charge and informed that two ladies will come in the day time and that they should be provided with all the help needed. The caller hung up.

When Sachin came to the office Latika informed him about the call. Sachin asked if anything was mentioned about the kind of help the women were expecting. She denied. Later when everyone had been to the field they waited anxiously for the ladies from the head office. They were quite surprised when Shamsuddin turned up instead in the office.

"Hey man! What brings you here?" Sachin asked.

"I don't know myself, *Dada*. Nayanda told me to report here at 11:00 in the morning," replied Shamsuddin.

"Oh. But how did he reach you?" Latika asked.

"Yesterday evening he came looking for me in the bus stop. Luckily I was there," he answered.

"They could have easily left a message with me instead," Latika thought. Then she said to him, "You wait here till we get back to you."

"*Ho*." He replied and sat down in the hall.

Sachin sat down figuring out about the job that Nayanmoni wanted Shamsuddin to do whereas they were not looped in for it. Their quest was answered shortly.

Two ladies, from the Head Office, came to meet them. They looked professional and held an aura of authority within them. They were very soft spoken. They told Sachin that they were counselors and were here to counsel the victimized girl.

It was not very difficult for Sachin and Latika to figure out why Nayanmoni had asked Shamsuddin to come to office in the morning. Shamsuddin knew the house and could accompany the counselors there to meet the young girl. Latika briefed Shamsuddin about the work and shortly afterwards the ladies left with Shamsuddin in his rickshaw.

****

Sachin and Latika eventually sat down to discuss the matter after completing their work.

"Do you think the girl will agree to go to the police after counselling?" asked Latika.

"Maybe…..But what I am concerned about we know of two cases only. There might be many more unreported."

Latika looked at him and nodded thoughtfully.

"According to the national crime figures the millennium shows a steep rise in the crime against women and children, an alarming increase in the case of human trafficking to be precise."

"*Human trafficking*?" Latika thought hard. Her knowledge on the subject was negligible. She asked Sachin to elaborate on the topic.

"It's a transnational crime that is picking up pace with time. With so many new opportunities in all walks of life people are moving towards the metros and big cities for better livelihood. And this migration is not just limited to the educated mass but also the poverty stricken illiterate people from the rural areas of the country. These people are easily lured for good paying jobs in big cities and end up in traps of the Human traffickers."

He paused to look at Latika who was listening to him with conviction. He continued before she shot her questions at him.

"The term is "SLAVERY". Human Trafficking is the modernized version of it you can say. The victims are sold off as bonded labor, domestic workers or forced into marriages or prostitution by the traffickers. From one hand to another they are littered off like a commodity with no expiration date and subjected to all sorts of physically and sexual abuse that they hardly have any strength left to resist.

One of my photojournalist friends showed me few pictures of a rescued victim. The girl in the photo was just eight years old and worked as a domestic maid in a well to do family in Delhi. The child was abused for more than a year in the household before she was rescued. She had broken ribs, ear drum and bore a burnt mark of a press iron on her back. He said the child was so traumatized that even after her rescue she did not utter a single word. She finally broke down on seeing her mother. It's a horrific tale Latika and the picture of the girl still haunts me. "

Latika thought of the girl in Miyan patti. She said, "You know, the pregnant girl looked almost dead. Had her sister not been abducted she would not have spoken a word about her trauma."

"The girls are subject to sexual exploitation, physical abuse and mental trauma Latika that they almost loose their sanity! Sometimes they can't even mention their village name to their rescuers which makes it very difficult to reunite them with their families."

"But how do they fall prey to these traffickers?" asked Latika.

"The traffickers are mostly locals, either male or female, a neighbor or distant relative whose job is to target the victim. The women and children as young as five to seventeen years are victimized the most. They lure the victims on pretext of money, job or marriage."

"The girl mentioned she had eloped with her neighbor," Latika commented.

"Once the victims fall prey they are sold off to agents who further sell them to the probable buyers or other agents in Delhi which is considered as the national transit hub for the traffickers. And you know what? Our Guwahati is the transit base of the North east India which is the source point of the traffickers."

"Is it? I didn't know that. But why?"

"We are economically backward state and cheaper. West Bengal, Bihar, Manipur, Mizoram, Jharkhand, Chattisgarh too are targeted for this reason. If they are lucky they are rescued otherwise they continue to live their inhumane life till death. There is hardly any hope of these girls to reunite with their family if they are sold off the borders. There is a huge demand of Indian girls overseas especially in The Middle East to work as sex slave. Children are mostly trafficked to work as a bonded labor in factories, beggars, organ trade and even sexually exploited sometimes in the name of offering free education and food. However young girls are always in huge demand in trafficking."

"But what could cause the demand for such large deportation of women and children?" Latika asked.

"There are several reasons to it. Changing lifestyle is giving steep rise to working couples who usually demand full time domestic worker to look after the house and children. Locals are expensive whereas the trafficked girls and boys are cheaper and available full time. Thus the placement agencies come to picture. They are mushrooming in every nook and corner of the metros and strangely there is no law to abide them. As a consequence these agencies remain legally undetected. They put their demand to the agents who further intimate their local network in the economically backward states and thus hunt for the prospect start locally.

Trafficked girls are also forced into marriages in states like Rajasthan, Punjab, Haryana and Uttar Pradesh where there is shortage of brides due to female infecticide. However, in the name of marriage these girls are considered only as a sex commodity and forced into providing a male heir for the family. She is also subjected to sexual favors to other male members in the family and is even resold if the she does not meet their expectation. In the long run she ends up in brothels. Forced prostitution is another main reason for the girl trafficking. The victim girl by that time gives up all hopes of freedom and in most cases neither the family comes looking for her. The main cause is poverty and illiteracy. After some time the family too forget about her and carry on with their life's struggle." Sachin paused to check his watch. It was almost afternoon and they had been talking the whole day.

He said, "I am hungry."

Latika quickly placed an order at the local restaurant next doors. The guy arrived in no time and Latika collected the order. She emptied the packet of chicken noodles in two plates and called Sachin. They ate without wasting time. Latika thought of something and shared with Sachin in between her bites.

"You know what I figured out something. Can't we conduct awareness programs on trafficking to alert the people through movies? I am sure people would understand better."

"It's a good medium to make people aware however I doubt the success rate. You have seen the results yourself with the health camp. The turnout was so poor. And if you call them to watch movies based on their problem I doubt anybody would be interested. You see movies in our country are only meant for entertainment wherein people can fantasize a world he can never achieve," replied Sachin.

Latika picked the last strand of noodle from her plate into her mouth. "I agree with you. But there is no problem in trying at least. Maybe in long run we are successful. "

"You don't give up, do you? O.K we will try," replied Sachin.

Later Latika asked him, "I was wondering Sachin, why Assam is one of the source point. Unlike the North Indians our society has great respect for women folk and social evils like dowry and female infanticide are not prevalent here. Then why is girl trafficking so high here?"

"It's true that our society does not have these social stigmas attached unlike the other states of the country. However the females of our society are biased in many ways with the males. Although the Assamese women has a major contribution to work force both in the rural and urban sector yet they are deprived economically thus making them weaker sections of the society and dependent on the male counterparts. They are also refrained from any decision making body turning them vulnerable in the hands of males. So in a way we men are prejudiced.

Now comes the other factor, as you know, Assam has been facing economic depreciation due to the ongoing ethnic clashes, militancy, flood or other natural calamity and political instability. You see majority of people living in rural Assam are poor and work very hard for their bread and butter because of these factors. So they fall prey easily to these traffickers who win them by flashing some couple of rupees. And by the time these people get to know anything the girls are already sold making it impossible to trace.

"Huh!"

Sachin mocked her. The topic they have been discussing so far was too intriguing to keep track of the passing time. The volunteers have already started returning and they had to stop the discussion to attend them. Sooner they became busy with their roles in the office administration and the discussion was shelved for the time.

Chapter Twenty Three

Latika lay wide awake in her bed at night. She had been tossing and turning for over an hour now but sleep was the last thing that evaded her mind. She was thinking about the discussion she had with Sachin in the office. He had elaborated the facts and figures so nicely that she had no doubts about his adverse knowledge in the field.

Till now she had no knowledge about human trafficking but Sachin had explained everything brilliantly. She quickly made notes of it in her dairy. It was a practice she had been doing since childhood and it helped her to keep a tap on "To do things list". After she completed her writing work she stared blankly at the page in front of her. The date on the page caught her attention. It was the same day four years back when she had divorced Siddharth.

"Siddharth" the name had once been her world. She had been in a relationship with him for almost seven years before taking the matrimonial vows. Of course after living-in with a partner for almost seven years marriage comes naturally. At least that's what she had thought. But Siddharth, a neo age Haryanvi Jat from Rohtak, thought otherwise. Although he wanted to pursue the relationship with her yet when it came down to final commitment he fled off to his family. His family was totally against his decision and succeeded in changing his mind. He was almost on the verge of marrying another girl of his parent's choice when he thought of meeting Latika one last time. And this time when he came down to see her in Delhi he did not let any second thoughts cross his mind. They secretly tied the knot in an Arya Smamaj temple with their friends as the witness.

Latika's parents knew about her relationship with Siddharth and they were against it from the very beginning but when Latika told them about her final decision they did not question further and flew down to Delhi to bless the new couple. It was an odd situation as Latika knew deep down in her heart that she will never be accepted by her in-laws whereas Siddharth was lovingly accepted as the son-in-law by her parents. Her parents had tried to convince Siddhrath's parents but all their efforts were in vain. Siddharth's parents had openly declared that they had disowned their son which had left Siddharth very disheartened.

Latika and her family supported him completely during that phase and Siddharth gained his confidence back but somewhere at the back of his mind he always remained disturbed by his loss due this alliance. And it kind of irked him to see Latika happily spending time with her family while he had been disowned by his own. This was the starting of their breakup. Once Latika's parents were gone, Siddharth started misbehaving with her. He would yell at her or start an argument on slightest provocation. It was the first time Latika saw him in this new avatar. Earlier she thought it was because he was feeling low for his family but then much later she realized that it was his character that she had never come across during their courtship period.

It was another face of Siddharth that she was discovering after marriage. The playful, supportive, caring and liberalized man had changed into a ruthless, prejudiced, egoistic, dominating husband. The change was gradual though yet the man she had loved so much did not seem to exist anymore. It started affecting his performance in the office too and down the line he lost his job. Latika still supported him both emotionally and financially. But things started falling apart. Siddharth who was one of the most promising students during his MBA days was now a jobless person due to his irritable behavior. No matter how hard he tried his reputation made it impossible for him to seek job in Delhi and NCR areas whereas Latika continued ascending the ladder of success in her work place. This was also a major cause of rift between the two and they quarreled over petty issues. Slowly their personal conflict crossed the bedroom door and reached the public place. They would spat just about anywhere. Once during a dinner party at a friend's place they had a heated argument and Siddharth hit her in front of all the guests. That night Latika did not go back home. She stayed at her friend's place crying all night. She had never dreamt in her life that Siddharth would change like this. She decided then and there that things had soured beyond repair between them and separating ways is the best solution.

Next day when she reached home she found the door locked. She opened the door with the spare key and found that neither Siddharth had returned home the previous night. She went to her bedroom and started packing her belongings then thought of waiting for Siddharth for a final meeting. That day Siddharth did not return. The following few days too he did not show up either. She tried reaching him on phone but his cell phone was switched off. She was anxious and angry at his inappropriate behavior. She was still calling him names when the door bell rang one morning. Thinking it to be Siddharth she ran to open the door. It was a courier boy who stood with an envelope addressed to her. The boy handed her the envelope and left. Latika tore the envelope seal and took out the letter from it. It was a divorce petition from a lawyer's office already signed by Siddharth.

Latika held the document tightly in her hand as tears rolled down her eyes. Never in her life had she imagined Siddharth would do away with her in this manner. At that particular moment she wanted to hold on to him forgetting all the differences they had had for the past few months. And then she had made a nasty decision. She decided to go back to Siddharth. It was not very difficult to trace him out as she came to know from his friends that he had gone back to his family in Rohtak. Latika jotted his Rotak address from one of his diaries and boarded the next bus to that city.

She knew she would not be welcomed there yet she wanted to give a last chance to their relationship. When the bus stopped in the Rohtak depot she got down from it wandered aimlessly on the roads. She checked in a hotel first and then went to his house. Siddharth's parental home was way off from the city in a village. Surprisingly his mother had welcomed her inside the house and treated her well. She too was unhappy that her son had taken such a decision but she told her that there is nothing she could do about it. Latika also came to learn that the real setback came from Siddharth's uncle and his family who held repute in the community. And according to them Siddharth had already committed a big mistake by going against his parent's wishes and as a punishment and lesson for the other young lads of the community he would remain an outcast as long as he was associated with Latika.

Latika finally got a chance to meet this uncle of Siddharth the next morning. He was an old man clad in dhoti-kurta with a white starched turban on his head with a matching thick moustache occupying a good portion of his cheeks. He sat at ease on a charpoy in the courtyard smoking hookah. Few more eminent family members shared the picture with him. Latika felt helpless standing in the middle with all eyes upon her. For the first time she felt how a veil came to rescue under such a circumstance. Siddharth was nowhere in sight. She had not succeeded in meeting him so far although she had left her hotel address with his mother. The men started questioning her.

She answered them as politely as she could but at heart she knew none of her answers would satisfy them any way. She had all her hopes on Siddharth who finaly made an appearance when the elders summoned him. But her hopes faded away when he clearly stated that he would not desert his family for Latika. He was ready to divorce her instead.

But Latika stick to her decision. With her tearful eyes and authentic pleas she managed to beg favours. Luckily the elders came to her rescue over Siddharth's statement. According to their verdict, marriage is not a fluke that could be reverted to convenience, so even though Siddharth had married against their wish he should give his marriage one more chance.

One month is all they gave them to sort out differences but with an additional clause that Siddharth cannot meet his family during this period. The decision was welcomed by Latika but denied by Siddharth. He was ready to give another chance to his marriage but did not accept the term of not meeting his family. His uncle clarified the stand saying that family has not accepted Latika as the daughter-in-law and to respect the institution of marriage Siddharth is given a chance. So he has to accept their terms. Siddharth managed to convince them a little in his favour and they allowed him to stay in the outhouse of their ancestral property. Siddharth looked at his mother who was eyeing everything from behind the door. He knew instantly that her pleas will reach deaf years. So he agreed to their terms. They were shown the outhouse and informed that next month same day the family will assemble once more to hear their decision.

Latika thanked her stars for this opportunity. She wanted to save her marriage at any cost. She checked out of the hotel and came to stay in the outhouse with Siddharth. It was a new beginning she thought and prayed everything turns out right. But this inning was much different than she had estimated.

Latika broke the silence once they were alone. "I am sorry Siddharth if I had hurt you. Believe me it had been hell for me too. I always wanted the best for you and I know you believe me. I have come to you forgetting all the past. Please let's give it a chance. "

"Why did you come here? Don't you see I have lost everything after marrying you and I shall never get it back as long as I am married to you? You can stay here as much as you want Latika, but my decision shall never change. I cannot live with you anymore," urged Siddharth.

"Why does the situation have to be so harsh always? We have spent seven years together don't you see that. Never before did we face a situation like now. Why Siddharth? What has changed so much in just three months after marriage?" cried Latika.

"I cannot leave my family and given the choice after marrying you I shall choose them to you. Now and always. "

"But Siddharth where is my fault here. I have always loved you and shall also love your family as you do then where is the problem?"

"The question is not about loving my family, Latika. That I know very well you will do but the question is acceptance. You see they are not ready to accept you. I don't know if that is possible or not," he replied. For the first time in months she saw him feeling something for her. She didn't need any more assurance from him for his love. His love for her had not died after all. He was weaning for his family only and way too much disturbed because of that.

Latika understood from the conversation that her challenge remain in winning the heart of his family this time and be gradually accepted but she didn't know how.

For the rest of the weeks she devoted herself completely to prove herself but at the end of each day she was back to square one. Siddharth was not supporting her at all and her fight was alone. She was a city girl and scrambled to her daily chores in village atmosphere each time. She was either pitied upon or laughed upon in her act to impress the family. They hardly saw her keenness in trying. All that mattered was she was an alien from an outer world here to pollute the innocent mind of the youngster. They somehow came to know of her live in relationship before marriage and considered her more or less a slut. They believed that with the couple around many young lads in the village would be instigated to follow their footsteps and defy the community. They always increased the gap which Latika tried to narrow.

However, there was another side of the coin too. While the living standard that disgraced Latika so much in the family somehow complimented her male beneficiary on all grounds. For that matter, according to their notion, it was alright for men to be in a live in relation prior to marriage or even if they have extra marital affair or pre marital sex for that matter. That was considered as some kind of manliness without much social stigma. Nobody questioned a man but a woman is disgraced if she is even found alone with the man she is distained to marry. Siddharth's society was no different in that matter. Thus in the scenario it was Latika who was considered the culprit by the community and it turned out to be the major setback in Latika's acceptance. She had never imagined that such casual lifestyle in metros was so much looked down upon and unacceptable by the society in smaller towns. She was frightened to think upon how her family and community would react if they even came to know about it as she too belonged to a conservative society. And above all how will her parents take these allegations on their child. The thoughts alone made her sweat. She had never confronted her family about it. For they knew she stayed in a paying guest accommodation and that's about it. Sharing a flat or for that matter a bed with a man prior to marriage would have been a shock for them too. They might be liberal enough but it was a sin that a daughter cannot commit. However in Delhi she and Siddharth had stayed together for seven years and that too in different leased apartments but nobody had questioned her modesty ever. Everything had been so cool. Her friends, colleagues knew about her status and it did not change their attitude towards her in any way.

But here she was getting pushed around by everyone in the community while she was pinning all her hopes on Siddharth. But his "Leave me out of it" behavior was not supporting her anyways. He had clearly mentioned that his family means everything to him and it was Latika's fight literally. Little by little she was losing faith and then one day came the final blow.

Someone in Siddharth's family openly said, "Did your parents teach you to sleep with men before marriage?" It pinched in her heart like a sharp edge knife and tears rolled down her eyes. So far she had faced their humiliation with dignity but when they pointed fingers at her parents she could not take it anymore. She ran to the outhouse and took out the divorce petition from her bag and signed it without any second thoughts. She kept it neatly stacked under the flower vase on the table and left the house without looking back. She returned to Delhi and moved out of the flat which they had shared for so long. Later she called up her parents to tell them she had filed for divorce.

The decision was a major setback for her parents and few days later her mother suffered a mild heart attack. Latika flew down to Guwahati and found the home front devastated after hearing her divorce. Her parents kept pestering her to change her decision but she kept mum. Her father even suggested flying down to Siddharth's family and convincing them but she denied him. Meanwhile her mother's health deteriorated and the doctor advised change of place might do better.

The three of them went to Kolkata to spend few days but the daughter's broken marriage could not revive the old lady and she breathed her last with another massive heart attack in Kolkata. Latika and her father returned home after finishing the last rituals and their life changed forever.

Latika held herself completely responsible for her mother's demise. Till date she had never forgiven herself. Their small family had shattered the moment she had revealed about her divorce. After her mother's demise her father had changed completely. He was so disheartened for the dual loss, first of his wife and second of Latika's marriage that he went in shock for several months after the incident. After Latika's departure from the house he felt so lonely and distressed that he was almost on the verge of losing his sanity. He had stopped socializing and hardly spoke to anybody in the neighborhood and always kept to himself. Slowly he started forgetting things. He would often forget to switch off the lights at night or close the main gate or switch off the gas stove. Skipping meals was a routine. And one day he even forgot his way home.

A neighbor called up Latika and told her about her father's condition. For the first time Latika realized how mean she had been all these years. She had never bothered to take the responsibility of her ageing parents. They always encouraged her but she hadn't realized earlier that they were not young anymore and looked upon her for emotional support. She had never even imagined how lonely her father would be after mother's demise and very selfishly she had told him about her return to Delhi. She was repenting that she hadn't asked him to come along. At least she would have been there to take care of him. Throughout her flight Latika wept. She didn't want to lose her father yet. She would go to any limits to make him happy. Few days later she brought her father along with her to Delhi and made sure to look after him completely. She fixed appointments with doctors and took good care of her father. Slowly with her sheer dedication and determination her father started showing signs of progress and in few years he was perfectly normal. This was the phase when she bonded with her father once more and till date he had been an eminent part of her life. And then when he finally disclosed his wish to go back to Guwahati and spend the rest of his life there she did not question him even once but made all arrangements to shift along with him forever.

She closed the notebook with a thud. She had come a long way since then and there was no looking back. Her priorities had changed over time and she found a new meaning to her life as a social activist. During her father's treatment the doctor had suggested her to take her father for group counseling. The sessions not only helped her father but also Latika to change her perspective towards life after her mother's untimely death and her divorce. She regained her lost confidence once more and took to life as it came. In one such session she befriended a lady who worked with an NGO for children development in the urban slum area in and around Delhi. With the lady's encouragement she joined in as a part time volunteer and found a new enthusiasm towards life. And from then on there was no looking back. Her life had found a new meaning helping these children. Later when she shifted to Guwahati she joined the NGO as a full time activist.

Chapter Twenty Four

"One, two, three......I shall count till ten and you can make a guess till then, O.K," said Prachi.

"Why whats the matter with you?" asked Latika.

"Stop asking questions. You are eating this laddu so guess what could be the reason for it." She replied rather playfully.

"How do I know? You brought it so I had it." Latika said with her mouth full.

"Oh don't be so mean. Come on at least try," pleaded Prachi.

"Forget her. I shall make the guess," said Sachin picking one laddu from the box. "Hmmm....Let's see. So your father has finally given the nod to your marriage."

Prachi hid her face in her palms.

"Am I correct," asked Sachin. Prachi simply nodded. And when she showed her face again she could not hide her smile. She was blushing like a young bride.

"Oooo…" Latika exclaimed and gave her a hug. "You little bitch. How come I didn't know about all these? Huh! "

Sachin picked up another Laddu, "Because mam, I was the one who lent her my shoulder every time she needed one. Guess what, Prachi's parents were dead against her choice as he happened to be in the Indian Navy. But I think this time they could not refuse her anymore."

"Absolutely! I am so thankful to you Sachin that you have always been there when I needed a friend," remarked Prachi.

"Always there for friends, mam," Sachin replied.

"But what is the whole story. I want to know too," said Latika.

"I met Manish in Bangalore and we hit upon right away. He serves in the Indian Navy. And when finally I told my parents about him they totally refused as they were against his profession. But I stick to my decision for the last two years. But this time when Manish came down to meet them they had to change their perspective. Now our parents are busy finalizing the wedding date," replied Parchi cheerfully.

"Wow! It's really good to know. So you are going to leave us very soon then. " Latika asked.

They chatted for some more time and then went back to their work. The news of Prachi's marriage was the hot topic of discussion for the next few days in the office. The volunteers, Sachin and Prachi would discuss on the venue for the honey moon destinations or wedding dresses or the jewelry or even the menu on the D- day while Latika usually joined them as a mute spectator.

Her own marriage experience was so sour that she didn't like to give any input out of fear. Watching Prachi's friends and family's participation in planning the event Latika realized what she had missed in her own wedding affair. Nevertheless she enjoyed participating as a mute spectator only and was amazed to find how different her emotions were now than it had been in Delhi.

****

One morning she woke up feeling very happy. It was a dream, a very sweet dream that she had never seen in all these years. It evoked the feeling of need in her, need of companionship, feeling of being in love, a feeling of longingness. A pure passion that was driving her mad yet she was clueless about what or who the dream was about. She only had a vague memory of opening the door for someone. Who, what where? She had no idea. But whatever the dream was it left her too happy and yearning at the same time. She blamed it all to her office gossip which was making the rounds these days and tried to forget the whole thing.

****

She got a call from the police station. She reached the police station and found Shamsuddin already sitting there. They were called for identification parade. The officer told them to identify their assailant among the men standing in a row in the interrogation room. Shamsuddin scrutinized thoroughly and narrowed down to the fifth men in the row. The officer asked if he was sure to which Shamsuddin firmly nodded. Then Latika came forward and did her bit of survey but could not find her man in the group whom she had slapped earlier. She shook her head. The officer thanked them and reminded them that they will be called again.

On her way back Latika saw the girl from the Miyan patti sitting outside the O.C's room in the police station. She went to meetup the girl. The girl looked better than the other day. She smiled at Latika while her aunt Nafisa stood up to greet.

"What a surprise? What are you ladies doing here?" asked Latika.

"We have heeded to your advice, *Bidoh*, and taken the police help," replied Nafisa.

"Your neice looks much better too. In fact she looks happy," remarked Latika.

"Why not Latika *Bidoh*? It's my turn to punish them now," replied the girl with confidence.

Latika could not stop herself and hugged the girl. "I am so happy for you," she whispered in the girl's ears.

Later, Nafisa told Latika that her neice was taking counseling sessions which has helped boost up her self confidence. They had also enrolled her for a rehabilitation program which will enable her to be financially independent in the near future. Latika was very pleased to hear that. She filled up with pride herself to be associated with an organization that really went out of the way to help people. At her heart she thanked God.

But when the girl asked her about her younger sister's search progress Latika was tightliped. She could only answer that a search team had gone to fetch her sister and they would very soon hear from them. The girl nodded cheerfully. She had no doubts that those people would bring back her sister safe and sound. She thanked Latika once again for all their efforts. But the question troubled Latika to the core of her heart. It's been half of the month and they were still not aware what was going on. She wanted to talk to Debjyoti and Nayanmoni regarding it.

****

Latika was tired of calling Debjyoti and Nayanmoni for the past two days but there was no response from the other end. However, that didn't deter Latika from her focus. She tried to take help the other way. She called up her friend in Delhi who worked as the volunteer with the NGO for child health development in the urban slums. She reffered Latika to another person who was associated with an NGO that worked on human trafficking cases. Latika talked to him at length regarding her case. He asked her to send in some details regarding the case. Latika collected as much details she could lay her hands upon without anybody's knowledge in the office and mailed to him. He replied he would call back when he gets a lead. There was nothing much she could do but wait. Back at office she knew very well that she had violated the protocol but she was ready to face the consequences.

Two days passed by and still there was no news from the guy. Latika was losing patience. She was no more interested in the office gossip and looked anxious. She tried calling up Debjyoti and Nayanmoni again but as usual there was no response. She didn't know why she was turning so restless. Was it the anxiety of not being in the field or nothing

179

challenging in her life. Coming to office in the morning and going back home in the evening didn't appeal to her anymore. She felt as if she would burst out of desperation.

That night almost around midnight she got a call from the NGO guy. He said that they had got a lead and were working on it. Most probably they would successfully trace the missing girl. Latika breathed a relief. Just the thought of it calmed her down. She smiled at herself as she had a definite answer now. That night she slept peacefully.

Next morning she went with Shamsuddin to visit the girl in the Miyan patti, very much aware of the fact that it was a big No-No for her. But she didn't let that bug her more than a second. She was on unofficial visit and nobody could stop her now. The moment she crossed the wooden bridge her anxiety subsided. Firstly, it was her home ground and secondly, she found a drastic change in the attitude of the people in the area. They recognized her instantly and were greeting her with a smile. She could not believe her stars and nodded at them in return.

She reached Nafisa's house and went inside leaving Shamsuddin to wait outside. This time she met Nafisa's husband too who was all praises for her and her NGO. She told them the good news about their missing girl and assured that she would be traced shortly. The couple thanked her again and again for all the support their organization was giving. They even told her that the two counselors visit the girl quite often which has helped the girl considerably. Latika also came to know that the girl was enrolled for a beauty parlor course under a rehabilitation program which the girl was looking forward to after her delivery. Latika expressed them her good wishes and left.

On her way back she questioned herself about the rehabilitation program that the girl was enrolled in. Nowhere in her mind could she think of beauty parlour training as the appropriate option for the girl who belonged to a very economically backward and conservative family. Latika thought of visiting the Head Office sometime and speaking to them about it.

****

It was late afternoon and Latika was finishing off her work in the office. Her mobile rang. She picked up the phone and saw it was her aunt, Snehlata calling. She answered the call rather surprised as Snehlata had never done that before.

"What is it *Pishi*? Is everything O.K?" She asked.

"No, Latika. I just came to know that Monidi is no more." Her aunt replied in a sad tone.

"Oh! That's too bad. When did it happen?" She asked.

"This morning. Her tenants called me up. They were also not sure of the exact time as nobody was in the house at that time. The poor soul had no one to turn to for help. I was so disturbed by the news that I called you up." She said.

"Have they informed her children?" Latika asked.

"I don't know Latika but I hope they have. I am leaving for Shillong in about an hour. I shall know about the situation there. At least I can be present in her last journey." The old lady sobbed.

"*Pishi* I shall come along too. Is it fine?"

"Fine."

She informed Sachin about the incident and rushed home. She quickly packed her bag and took her father's leave. In about an hour they were on their way to Shillong once more. Snehlata was sobbing throughout the journey and Latika consoled her. They reached Monidi's house by late evening.

The house gave a deserted look. Some of her relatives had come over. Her dead body lay on the floor covered in white piece of cloth. An earthen lamp lit near her dead body. She seemed like resting yet her facial expression spoke of the pain she must have been though during her last moment. Her funeral was postponed till the next morning as her children were on their way home from the different cities and could not make it before the next day.

Snehlata sat down quietly in a corner of the room along with other women folk. She thought of the moments they had shared together all these years. Never had she imagined that someone so close could have such a lonely and agonizing death. What irked Snehlata most was the lady had done so much for her family yet no one was near her at the time of her death. If the tenant had not come looking for then Monidi's dead body would have remained unattended for hours or maybe days. Snehlata sobbed endlessly at the very thought of it while Latika tried to console her.

Next morning in her children's presence Monidi's body was taken for last rites after completing all the rituals. Tally of friends and relatives followed her body to the pyre in the cremation site. Tragically many of them disdained from visiting her when she was alive yet they came to mourn her death.

Whatever Latika saw strained her heart more. She had heard so much about the demised lady from her aunt that she felt she knew Monidi quite well. Just few days back they had sat together in the hall discussing her special cookies.

How lively the lady was and yet how sad she sounded sometimes. Tears dropped down Latika's eyes mercilessly thinking about Monidi. She hugged her aunt in reassurance.

They spent some time with the family members encouraging them to keep faith in God's will and stayed in the house for another night before returning back to Guwahati. Their journey back was more or less silent. None of them spoke on the way home. Latika dropped her aunt at her house and wished her to pull through well in this hard time. Her aunt thanked her and went inside. The cab drove off towards Latika's house.

Chapter Twenty Five

It was Sunday morning and Latika had all the right to wake up late. She drowsily looked at the wall clock which showed quarter to eight. She still had some more time to stretch herself in the bed. Outside she could hear her maid working while her father sat in the verandah reading the newspaper. No office today she thought for she didn't wanted to meet anybody after coming back from Monidi's funeral. The last two days had been too stressful for her. She wondered how her aunt was feeling. Just previous night they were back together from Shillong. Her mind was still preoccupied by the thoughts of Monidi and she felt sad.

Her phone buzzed and she picked it up to see the caller. It was Sachin. She got up hastily to take the call feeling there must be something important.

"Hello?"

"Hi, I called up to say we are meeting at Nayanmoni's place for lunch. Reach there by 11:00 a.m ok," he said.

"Why what's the matter?" she asked.

"Check the paper. I am sending you his address. Don't be late ok," saying he hung up.

Latika kept looking at the phone. Without any intimation her heart beat escalated. She felt an urge to meet Debjyoti after hearing the news of their return. It had been more than ten days since she had last seen him and almost weeks since they had last spoken.

"Damn." A voice inside her said. She shook her head violently. "This had to be with the new project" she reminded herself although deep down she knew the feeling was different.

She got out of her bed and rushed out to the verandah. She grabbed the paper from her father's hand.

"What's wrong with you? You could simply....." Her father snarled.

"Sorry, *Bapi*. Just a second. I will give it back right away." She quickly ran her eyes through the whole pages but could not find anything that could hold her attention. She returned the paper to the old man and ran inside where the stack of old paper was kept. She went through the pages quickly of the last two days paper. And in the second page of one of them she found what she was looking for. A small snippet in a column of the page gallantly mentioned the efforts their NGO in rescuing a young girl from the clutches of human traffickers. The news highlighted the plight of the girl who was missing from her house in the city since past fifteen days.

She kept the paper neatly back in the stack and hurried to get ready. In about an hour she was on her way to Nayanmoni's house. Her excitement reached a new level as she pedaled the accelerator of her car through the busy streets. She had to stop many times to confirm the address from the passerby. Nevertheless she managed to reach his place in the specified time. His house was in one of the finest locality of the city, Uzan Bazar. She stopped her car in front of the house. It was a beautiful Assam type house with a big lawn and flower beds in the front with the entrance overlooking the mighty Brahmaputra. She liked it instantly.

She went inside the gate and rang the door bell. A beautiful lady in her early thirties opened the door. She was wearing a contrast Mekhla that complimented her flawless fair skin and jet black eyes. Latika assumed her to be Nayanmoni's wife.

"Hello mam! Has everybody come?" asked Latika.

The lady smiled and nodded, "*Ho*. Please come inside."

Latika found the house incredibly beautiful inside as well. She could not stop herself from complimenting the interiors as she followed the lady. They stopped in front of a room and the lady asked Latika to go inside. Latika shoved the door curtain aside and peeped in. It was a spacious room with very limited furniture and its rear door wide open to the backyard. Prachi was easing herself on the rug spread across the floor in the middle of the room while Sachin occupied the arm chair next to the music system in one corner of the room listening to Bhupen Hazarika. The room echoed with the song

"O Ganga behti ho kyun...."

Latika waved at them and tip toed silently to the rug. She found them engrossed in the lyrics of the song. She looked around her surroundings. Beside the music system was a big wall rack with a big collection of CDs and cassettes. The other wall was occupied with books and had a small reading table in the corner. The room spoke of personal taste and was more or less a den where one could unwind easily. It had lots of space and privacy which Latika always yearned for. She waited for the song to be over.

"So guys I think I missed a lot in the last few days," said Latika.

"Yes mam, you did," replied Sachin. "You must have already read the news in the paper."

"Our big guys have done a great job and we are proud of them," added Prachi.

Latika nodded. "But where are they?" Her heart raced as she asked the question. The thought of Debjyoti's presence disturbed her.

"Here we are." Nayanmoni said from the doorway carrying a tray of snacks in his hand. Debjyoti followed him close behind with some glasses and a bottle of coke. They put the tray in the middle of the rug and seated themselves leisurely grabbing some throw cushions. For split of seconds she didn't know how to face him and thought of ducking for cover. But she overcame her thoughts and exchanged greetings with both of them as usual. She was glad that her hands were not shaking while taking the glass of coke that Debjyoti had offered. Sachin changed the CD to a new jazzy number and in moments the ripples of emotions within her subsided and she was normal. Her desire to hear about their whole operation and about the girl was put to rest by others.

"We have heard it n^{th} times already Latika. Not again please," laughed Sachin.

"Stop your pranks Sachin," snapped Prachi. "You know well why she was not here."

Latika knew it was not the appropriate time to ask so she waited to hear the story later. "Let the party roll," she said.

Sachin smiled at her. It was celebration time so they casually discussed everything other than work. While Nayanmoni and Debjyoti kept the snacks and coke rolling till the lunch was served. Finally Nayanmoni's wife summoned everybody at the dining table. Several Assamese cuisines were meticulously displayed on the table and the aroma set the appetizer burning. Everyone looked hungrily at the dishes.

"Latika I havn't introduced you to my wife," said Nayanmoni putting a hand across his wife's shoulders as he spoke, "She is Sujata, the anchor of my life. She is a T.V news reader. You must have seen her on the news channel."

Latika nodded. "I recognized her instantly. But it seems she is an excellent cook too."

"Sujata *ba* is excellent in her culinary skills no doubt but she is an excellent singer as well. And we won't go without hearing her sing," said Prachi.

"Oh you guys always flatter me. Now sit down and have lunch," said Sujata smiling.

After lunch once more everybody assembled in the room and occupied the rug while Sujata crooned in her beautiful voice with the keyboard. Sometimes Nayanmoni also accompanied her. Time simply passed by and everybody was unaware of the dark clouds overcastting the sky. By evening it already appeared dark outside.

By the time everybody set to go it started drizzling. They thanked the couple and rushed to reach home. Prachi left with Sachin in his bike and Latika offered a lift to Debjyoti in her car till the interstate bus stand as he had to go to Shillong. By the time they reached the bus stand it started raining heavily.

"Are you sure you want to go there in this weather? It's going terrible every minute," said Latika as she halted the car outside the building.

"I have to anyway. Thanks by the way," replied Debjyoti and got off the car. Within minutes his clothes were wet as he rushed inside the building for cover. Latika thought of waiting sometime just to ensure he was fine. It was pouring very heavily and the streets started water loggin. A little later Latika started the engine and made homewards but by the time she reached the corner of the road the scenario was pathetic as the streets were water logged with knee deep water. Her intuition made her call Debjyoti and he answered.

"I am not very far off yet. You want me to pick you up. I see the streets down with knee deep water."

"I won't say no. The bus service is halted due to heavy rains in Shillong. So I don't think I can make it today," he replied.

"Ok I am on my way." Latika replied. She took a U-turn and in few minutes halted outside the interstate bus depot. Debjyoti came out running and hopped in the car. He was wet as a cat.

"Sorry about that. I could not help." He smiled at her.

"It's ok. I can drop you at your place," she said.

"That would be great," he grinned.

They drove towards zoo road which was at the other side of the city. The scene was similar there too. Debjyoti grew little worried as he knew the area near his home would be quite flooded by now. He insisted Latika to drop him on the main road and go back but she found it very unethical as it was already dark and raining heavily.

"You might be electrocuted on the road itself if you get down here." She demanded. "Keep sitting and I shall drop you in some safe place near your home."

"O.K" He sat sternly looking at the road ahead. The car's speed lowered as the visibility was difficult due to the heavy downpour. After almost an hour of struggle on the main road she reached the lane that lead to his apartment. She stopped the car in front of the lane. There was no electricity and the lane looked like a dark alley. Debjyoti opened the car door to get down but Latika insisted that she would take the car below his apartment building which was at the end of the lane.

"Its ok. I can manage," Debjyoti insisted.

But Latika won't listen. "Even if I keep the car lights on you will not be able to see the road beyond a couple of meters in this darkness. If I can drive till this point I don't mind a few more meters." Latika argued.

"I don't think it's a good idea because you might get stuck in this narrow lane." Debjyoti warned her.

"I can reverse my car in the parking facility in your apartment." Latika replied and kept driving ahead. As Debjyoti had said earlier the lane narrowed down after some meters and due to lower elevation the water touched the base of the car. It hit something with a thud and the engine stopped. Latika tried to restart but it won't.

"Oh my God what do I do now?" She sounded concerned. She tried few more times but the car won't take a start. Anxiety showed on her face as she meddled with the car keys.

Debjyoti read her anxiety and to calm her down suggested that she should come out with him to his flat and wait till the rain stopped.

"Once it stops raining the water will recede and I can get help too for pushing the car." His suggestion looked obvious to her as there was no point sitting in the car. They got down from the car and ran towards the apartment in the dark surrounding. Latika was drenched in a minute. She followed Debjyoti's footsteps as much as possible but as the terrain was new to her she fell down helplessly in one of the potholes. Debjyoti helped her up but she had sprained ankle. She walked with a limp the rest of the lane as he held her close for support.

Somehow she managed to reach his flat and fell flat the moment he withdrew his support to open the door. He held her in time in his grip and swept her off her feet as they entered his abode. It seemed ages since they were together so close and all to themselves. The situation was quite odd yet they both seemed to enjoy it. It had been months since they had had their casual talk or let alone even had the opportunity to be alone. Even in Nayanmoni's place they acted too formal with each other. Yet in Shillong spending few hours together in the trek brought them so close.

"Let me down." She snapped as she struggled in his embrace.

"Hold on lady! I have decent neighbors." He muted and gently lowered her on the couch. She broke free from his clutches and snarled up in a corner. The room was dark as in the outside but she could feel him standing right in front of her.

"You invited this but I am not gonna rape you." He quirked his eyebrows as he spoke.

"Fuck off and get some light." She hissed and she heard him go away. Some drawers opened and he reappeared with a candle in the room. The candle illuminated his facial expression as he placed it on a candle stand. He looked bemused with their sudden physical encounter.

He took a good look at her in the illuminated room. She looked terrified like a wet cat snarled up in the corner of the couch. He could not help smiling at her.

"Whats so funny?" She demanded.

"Nothing just ease down. I will go and change." Saying he disappeared inside.

Latika sat quietly clutching her wet dress. Surprisingly the odd situation she was in didn't pester her much. Infact her excitement grew a new level finding him so close to her. It seemed she had always wanted to be in a situation like this with him where they could be alone, just the two of them, to understand each other better and spend some time with each other. It was a feeling that had been haunting her past couple of months but she had always brushed the feelings aside thinking it to be ambiguous. She believed she had moved on and there is no space for these feelings in her life anymore. Yet she felt so much at ease in his flat clutching her wet dress and drenching his couch.

She diverted her attention towards the room. It was a contrast to what she had seen in Nayanmoni's place. Newspaper lay haphazardly on the chair, on another rested some of his clothes and in a corner an open bag still unpacked. Latika cringed at the sight of it. Too much boyish for a man of his age she thought. Debjyoti returned wearing a Tee and shorts rubbing his hair with a towel.

"I think you should also go and change unless you want to drench my couch too with your wet clothes on." He mocked at her.

"Its ok I can manage," saying she tried to get up from the couch but her sprained ankle gave way.

"You want me to help you getting off your wet clothes or you can manage yourself," he laughed off and sank down in the sofa. "Just take the right for the bathroom and I have left some clothes for you in the rack."

Latika quietly followed his instructions and limped slowly towards the bathroom. Once inside she closed the door with a bang. She struggled out of her wet clothes and wore his Tee and track pants that he had left for her. The smell of his body odor filled her with a new sensation of thousand spines poking at once. She hit herself for having such thoughts occupy her mind but could not stop herself. Annoyed with herself she opened the door and came out.

The room was vacant and she could hear Debjyoti in the kitchen. She sat quietly on the couch again. The rain water splashed against the windows and it was lightning outside. She wondered how long it would be before the storm ended. Infact she was worried about the storm of unwanted emotions within her which Debjyoti could easily read in her eyes. She diverted her attention to her father for he might be worried as she was not home yet. She thought of calling him and looked for her cell phone. She remembered leaving it in the dashboard of her car.

"Damn!" she cursed.

"What happened?" He asked as he placed two cups of tea on the table.

"I left my cell phone in the car. I wanted to call *Bapi* but now...." She was cut short.

"Call him from mine." He said handing her his cell phone.

"I don't remember the number....." She looked distressed.

"I have his. I have just now called him up and told him you are with me and I shall drop you home once the rain stops." He replied.

Latika was surprised to hear that. "You have *Bapi's* number? How come?"

"Why we keep talking to each other off and on. So?" He answered.

"How come?"

"Oh come on. Your old man is a good buddy of mine. Actually the night we spent together in the hospital we shared lots of things and thus keep in touch with each other. So if you want to speak to him you can. " He said.

Latika was puzzled. Her father had never spoken of him to her. Latika took the phone and called her father. He said that he too was in Snehlata's house and unable to go home due to rain. They talked briefly then hung up.

"All is well now? Come let's have tea," said Debjyoti.

Latika limped to the table and pulled a chair to sit down. Debjyoti eyed her closely in his clothes. She looked so much at home, fresh and naive. Her wet hair neatly tucked behind her ears had wander off slowly to her cheeks giving her a childish look. The faint candle light framed her almost irresistible as she sipped the tea from the cup holding it in between her palms. Debjyoti could not take his eyes off her. As if he wanted to capture her in this posture forever.

Latika looked at him over the rim of her cup and their gaze met. Something happened between them which sparked the hidden fire within. And the next moment Debjyoti stood holding her close to him cupping her face in his palms and searching wide in her eyes. He found his answer and drew her within as he lower his head to kiss her. As his lips lightly touched hers he felt her whole body shiver. He tightened his grip around her holding her close, feeling her heat, her heart beat while she gently placed her arms around his neck drawing him close, feeling his body heat and temptation. Her lips parted in reciprocation and their tongue met. She could feel him inside her now draining her, wanting her like never before. Their need aroused. Something which she had withheld for all these years was about to unleash taking her to a new heights, a feeling of belongingness and completeness.

The time had stopped clicking. His tongue searched for her, tasting her, feeling her, enjoying her. His hands slid past her neck to her back thrusting her more towards him while with the other hand he smothered her hair as he suckled her. With each moment his urgency grew and he fought to control himself. He was startled to find himself so much wanting her. She was appealing to him from the very day he saw her yet he had distanced himself from her. He had fought his emotions many times over in the past but now he wanted to give way, take in what was appropriately his. She was giving him as much as he was demanding and he wanted to keep it that way but he did not want it to be a one night stand although he could see that coming easily. He wanted her completely not in halves. His grip slightly lightened with the thought and Latika sensed it immediately. Before he could do anything she broke free maintaining a considerable distance between them.

Once she was out of his zone her neurons started working. All she thought at that moment was how cheap she must have looked melting in his arms, begging him. She had shamelessly allowed him to know her feelings. He must be thinking of her as whore who would drive down to someone's flat on a rainy day and change into his clothes and desperately show him how lonely she had been all these while. The thoughts disturbed her so much that she was furious with herself. Her cheeks blushed and tears rolled down her eyes. She had ruined her own modesty to the man she had fallen for. "Fallen for?" She rephrased it in her mind once more. "Have I fallen in love with him or is it just infatuation." The thoughts tore her apart and in the confusion she hid her face in her palms.

Debjyoti looked at her in dismay. What a fool he had been he thought. He had blindly hurt the woman he loved. Just few seconds ago she seemed all his but what had happened now. What had he done so terrible to hurt her so badly that she was weeping. She must have thought of him as an opportunist rather than a lover. A sex starved maniac who brought girls over to fulfill his lust. "Oh my God what have I done?" He thought and moved away from her.

Chapter Twenty Six

Latika stood alone in the room. In few minutes she had composed herself. She was not going to let anyone make a fool of herself even if it meant distancing herself from the person she had fallen for. She stood facing the window looking at the gush of rain water beating against the glass pane. She had already bore the bruise of loving someone and it took her four years to revive. She was not very keen on listening to her heart again which had shamelessly displayed her feelings for this man just a few minutes ago. Moreover how much she knew about him? Probably he was married and had an adorable wife. What if his wife barged in and sees a woman in her husband's clothes? Although the chances seemed negligible as the unkempt room hardly spoke of any women's presence and she had already marked a single toothbrush in his bathroom cabinet. But that does not mean he didn't have a wife. Probably she was out of station and Latika filled with guilt to have chanced upon her absence in this way.

She turned back to escape the turmoil within and saw Debjyoti looking at her. He was standing across the table maintain a considerable distance in-between. His face was clearly visible in the candle light that held the expression of remorse. He assumed he had done something terrible and could never be forgiven yet he begged for forgiveness.

"I am sorry." He said. "I didn't mean to offend you in anyway. I never meant to hurt you but I am terribly sorry."

Latika was startled to hear that. She could not understand why he was saying that. It was her fault she thought as she was the one who had led him onto a situation like this. She could have left him over in the bus stop rather than come over to his place. She should be the one begging for forgiveness.

"No. I am sorry." Her voice trailed off as she spoke the words. He heard it to his dismay but didn't utter a word. It was better to keep mum he thought. Silence engulfed them as none spoke. Only the storm outside crackled against the window sometimes. Latika's sprained foot ached and she hopped back to the couch. Debjyoti left the room once again. He didn't want to distract her and thought it would be better if he remained out of sight as long as they were confined in his flat.

His phone buzzed. Latika had kept it on the couch when she had made a call to her father. As she happened to be sitting near it she picked the phone in her hand. The caller name "Kuki" displayed on the screen of the handset. Debjyoti came over and she handed him the cell phone. He took the call and spoke to the caller while moving out of the room. Latika almost heard the conversation at his end but she could not understand as he spoke in a different language. Probably his wife had called she thought as he sounded very happy taking the call and later she heard him ending it up with kisses.

Latika felt something sting in the heart. "Just a few minutes back he was kissing me!" she thought. Pangs of agony engulfed her and made it unbearable for her to stay in his flat any longer. She thought it would be stupid enough to sit back on his couch waiting for the rain outside to stop. Rather she should go and wait outside and probably may get a lift. She rose and limped to the main door without making any sound. She thought it would be easier to disappear before he knew. She walked out of his flat and closed the door behind. Darkness in the staircase frightened her. But it didn't stop her from wading down the stairs holding on the railing. But her sprained ankle gave way and she cried out in pain. Debjyoti heard her and came out running only to find her struggling down the stairs in the darkness.

Gush of fury flooded him as he ran down to her and without any second thought picked her up in his arms and brought her back inside the flat. He was nowhere close to gentleness as he dumped her once more on the couch with a thud. She could hear him breathe heavily as he stood right in front with his eyes piercing at her.

"What do you think you were doing there?" He snarled at her.

Latika was still gasping for support as she tried to sit up. Everything happened so suddenly that she had no time to think. All she thought was getting out of his place away from him.

Her silence made him lose his temper and he grabbed her arms and made her stand up facing him. "Answer me." He demanded.

She gathered all her strength to break free but when she could not. She looked into his eyes and replied sternly, "I wanted to leave."

"Why? What's wrong here?" He asked angrily still holding onto her.

It was lightening outside and in the flash their eyes met for few seconds. They were both spitting fire at each other.

"I can't stay here with you any longer." She answered abruptly.

Fear of rejection infuriated him further and in the turmoil his nails dug into her skin hurting her but he stood unaware.

"You think I will pounce upon you?"

"You are hurting me!" She retaliated and he withdrew his hands off her arms.

She dropped down on the couch instantly while he stood looking down at her. His arrogance made her burn with fury within and she spit back in vengeance.

"You think I am the kind of women who want no strings attached and flirt with married men when their wife is away. Just because I came to your empty flat and changed into your clothes you figured out she is easy. Right?"

Her statement irked him. She typified him indirectly. He didn't like it though he controlled his outburst. Rather he gently stooped over her and whispered.

"Whatever made you think I liked women with no strings attached or the type of husband who would flirt around when his wife is away?"

She sensed his change of tone but did not allow herself to be humiliated anymore. She shoved him back to his position and distanced herself.

"Weren't you flirting with me a few minutes back?" She reasoned him. Then paused to add, "And your wife is not around."

Her answer set his heart racing to a new beat. He never imagined his marriage would be of so much concern to her that she was ready to defy him even in the present circumstance. He easily figured out how less she knew about him. His fear vanished instantly and so did his temperament. Nevertheless he got his answer from her fears which she had disclosed so innocently. And he was glad to know that they were genuine. He had no doubts about how she felt for him but he wanted her to overcome her inhibition first. So he eased down and allowed her to take time. He backed off from her and sat on the sofa opposite her with his eyes still glued upon her.

She tried to stirred clear off his gaze. It annoyed her more to see his composed self as it made him very unpredictable and she didn't want to let down her guard. She could easily make out from the amusement in his gaze that she had hinted something which he was too quick to pick up and was now happy to roll the ball in his court.

"Stop looking at me like that." She snapped.

A smile appeared on his lips as he said, "Oh Latika! Why do you always have to be on guard? Let your hair down once and see it's not that bad a world after all. Everybody has his/ her share of ups and downs in life but that doesn't mean we should stop hoping." He still held her gaze.

His wordings puzzled her. She asked, "What do you mean?"

Debjyoti knew it was coming and he was prepared for it. "I mean why not give our self a chance. Who knows maybe we are destined for it. " He paused to see her reaction. She was prying him with suspicion. She took her time to digest what he had proposed.

"Are you suggesting we could start an affair and see?" She quirked her eyebrows as she spoke. He nodded. "And what about your wife?"

"She is not here. So don't bother." He claimed easily.

She could not believe what she just heard. She felt humiliated again. She rose to leave saying, "Wow! What a thought. I think we are past the age when we take life hany panky. So Mister I better leave you alone to your proposition." She started walking towards the door. But he stopped her midway.

"Get off my way. I don't want to speak to you anymore." She said furiously. But he stood blocking her way.

"I am not done yet. It's true that we are mature enough to understand our responsibilities and priorities but should that mean turn a blind eye to our own feeling. " He said politely with much thoughtfulness.

"I don't feel anything for you!" she snapped at him though at heart she knew pretty well that she was lying. But she didn't want to lose her dignity after what he had proposed.

He was waiting for that answer. "Oh really! I can prove it right away," he said stepping forward to minimize the distance between them but refrained from touching her.

Latika backed off immediately nevertheless he was still crowding her. He took notice of it and this time continued rather seriously, "Latika I have no shame to admit my feelings for you. No matter how hard I tried I could not stop myself from getting attracted to you. But I don't want to force myself onto you. You have the liberty to make your decision. What I am concerned is don't lock yourself up for what had happened in the past. Let go and get on with your life." He paused and backed off.

Latika stood speechlessly looking at him. It was an honest confession straight from his heart that made her heart twinge. There was something in his voice that touched her heart immediately. All her logic fell flat when her heart won over her brain and she knew it would be difficult to hold her back further. He had already admitted his feelings for her and she had never before realized how much she yearned for him too but she refrained from confessing.

He continued without looking at her, "I wanted you know this before I leave. But trust me I never thought of confessing to you in such a circumstance. I promise not to bug you again but you must wait till the rain stops. It ….. "

Latika cut short his words, "You are leaving?"

He turned back to look at her. She looked confused. "Didn't you know?"

"What?" She asked in sheer disbelief.

"Maybe you didn't get the update as you were out of station. I am going to Delhi next week as I have been assigned a new project. Nayan has taken over as the new team leader in the office yesterday." He paused. Then rephrasing his lines said in almost a whisper, "So you won't have the trouble of facing me anymore which I know would have been difficult for you."

She could not figure out what to say. Suddenly everything seemed to fall apart. Just a few minutes ago he was taking about their relationship and now he spoke of never facing her again. A lump in the throat made it impossible for her to speak and a tear dropped down the corner of her eye. She was quick enough to wipe it off with the back of her hand. All her barriers broke making her vulnerable. She felt the soil beneath her feet slipping off. Never before had she experienced such feeling, not even when Siddharth openly told her that he would never come back. The fear of losing Debjyoti now grew so strong within her that without any warning her eyes overflowed and tears poured out. Unable to control any further she let herself in and hugged him tight.

Debjyoti held her close as she sobbed in his arms like a school child whose favorite toy was taken back. He caressed and smoother her hair as she dug her head deep in his chest wetting his Tee. He kept planting sweet kisses on her head till she regained composure. Finally she held her head high and looked up in his eyes while her body lay tangled in his arms. Her moist eyes burnt with desire as she put her hands softly around his neck and gently pulled his head down to her lips.

She could feel his grip tightened around her as her lips met his. He drew her closer enough to let her breath as she showered him with her passion that he was yearning so badly. He led her on as she let her inhibitions wash away to his demands. They held each other passionately submitting themselves completely to each other.

And finally when it was over Debjyoti murmured in her ears softly, "Why do you always defy me? Can't you see how much it aches to withhold?" She snuggled back in his chest and let him caress her. Then he picked her up and laid her gently on the couch.

Chapter Twenty Seven

They sat close on the couch snuggling each other. Debjyoti kissed her again but it was more brotherly than passionate. He knew she was ready to give herself in but he didn't want to take her in this manner. He controlled back his desire to make love to her as he wanted it to be special. He didn't want it to be just a fling rather she should accept him with all his baggage. She had to know more about him to submit herself completely to him. He had already waited for so long that waiting some time more didn't make much difference to him. He held her hand in his and waited patiently for her to question him.

Latika sensed his dilemma and looked up at him. "What's bothering you now?" she asked.

Debjyoti read her for a moment then said, "Soon the rain will stop and you will be gone."

Latika put her feet down and replied playfully, "Let's pray that it rains all night then."

"But I want you to stay forever."

Latika looked at him longingly.

"Marry me," he proposed.

Her eyes bore suspicion. She didn't know how to react. He sounded so casual that she disbelieved him.

"I am serious Latika. I don't know how to put it across but I don't want to be lonely anymore," he said searching her eyes.

Latika thought for a while then asked, "Why are you lonely?"

Debjyoti held her gaze and replied, "Sangeeta is no more. I lost her to cancer two years back." His voice trailed off as he continued, "Life had not been easy for me after that incident all these years Latika. First I had to bear with her separation then Kuki's, our daughter. She was just two then and I could not handle her responsibilities alone and was bound to leave her at my parents care in Shillong. Since then I have been living a partial life Latika but I don't want to anymore. " He waited eagerly to hear her verdict. His heart beat was racing fast as if it would never stop galloping.

Latika looked at him silently. All these years she had thought she was the only one who suffered but in front of her sat a man who had faced the harsh realities of life just like her. She remembered how her life had taken a complete U-turn after divorce and how many sleepless nights she had had struggling to make her life a little better. She could never forget how lonely she had been when she had to tend to her ailing father. She could easily relate to his agony even if she was not present to share it at that time. She could now make out why he was amused when she was categorizing him as a womanizer and why he was so happy responding the call some time back that infuriated her so much. She was ashamed of herself of being so judgmental about him. She pressed his hands in reassurance and without speaking a word nodded her head in approval to his proposal.

Debjyoti hugged her close and murmur softly praying to her, "Thank you."

"No. Thanks to you. But you have to know about me too. I too ....." She murmured back.

"You don't have to tell me anything Latika." He whispered back. "I know about you." His answer surprised her. She had never mentioned anything about her past to anyone here and he was saying he knew everything.

He held her close and continued, "That night in the hospital I and your old man were riding the same boat. He was concerned about his daughter and I was praying for my love. Your old man somehow figured out my feelings for you and when he asked me I shamelessly admitted it. He was glad to know that there was someone else to care for his daughter. And then he told me all about your past while I told him about myself and Kuki. In the end he held my hand and said that he would be more than happy to see his daughter settled with me however the end decision was solely yours. So even if I and your old man wanted it you were the ultimate authority. I told him I would respect your decision under all circumstance. Since then Latika we spoke more often like buddies and talked about everything except you."

Latika's eyes were moist again. She had never known that her father knew her so well. Since childhood he had taken care of all her needs and wants yet he never made any attempt to influence any of her decisions. Although he knew about Debjyoti yet he never mentioned about him to her. Maybe he wanted her to realize it herself rather than get carried away by his suggestion. She loved her father more than ever now and wanted to reveal him her little secret as soon as possible. She looked out of the window and prayed the rain stopped sooner.

They held each other and Debjyoti showed her his daughter's pictures on his cell phone. She was his carbon copy and a cute little thing. He then started telling Latika about his little one's prank and how she longed for him to visit her more often.

"My heart aches each time when it's time to say goodbye to her. She clings to the window till I am completely out of sight and then broods over for days till I announce my next arrival again. She is so young Latika yet she has to bear the pain every time I go there. But I can't bring her here till I have someone to share the responsibilities. "

"We will do that together," Latika replied instantly and she knew deep inside that she would do anything to make the best of the chance life had given her again. Debjyoti sighed in relief. It felt as if a big load was lifted off him. All these years he had refrained from giving himself another chance with the sheer thought of his daughter but he always thought that with Latika by his side he can do better with his life. And now with her approval he felt safe and happy. He could not ask for more after that.

****

They were busy preparing some snacks and tea together in the kitchen. Latika felt so much at home doing the chore. Debjyoti had searched his closets for some hard drink for celebrating their new status but he could not find any. So they squared back to tea with some pakoras to go along with it. The combination was ideal for any rainy day.

"When are you leaving?" she asked as she flipped the pakoras in the pan.

"Most probably by Friday. Till then I shall spend some time with Kuki. She will be very upset to know that I will be gone for so many days," he replied. He thought for a while then suggested, "Why don't you come along too? It will be so much fun. " Even though he had said it he knew it was not possible for her take leave from the office.

"I wish I could but you know the possibility. How I wished we could spend some more time together? Had it not rained today you would have left without even thinking of me," she complained.

Debjyoti embraced her from behind and said laughing, "You are already complaining like a wife, sweetie and what made you think that I never thought of you." He turned her to face him and said, "Only God can tell you how I have missed you these twenty days. You didn't even bother to look at me when I was leaving. You had kept yourself hidden behind the computer that day. And when I came back from Delhi you were not there. I was so desperate that I had to literally fight myself from calling you up just to hear your voice. And then when we finally met today at Nayan's place you seemed so distant that I thought of some other time to meet you. I had never figured we would meet like this but I am so thankful we did. Now I can leave peacefully but you promise me that you will take care of yourself in my absence. Whatever be the circumstance you will not venture alone in the slum area. I mean it Latika."

Latika held his palms and pressed gently nodding at him. But Debjyoti looked more concerned. "Decca is still at large you see. He is the master mind in this girl's case. God knows how many more abductions he has carried in the slum. Few of his allies including the one who smacked you have been put behind bars. The ACP had promised to nab the others as early as possible. I shall go to the police head quarters tomorrow and get the latest update. He must be nabbed before I leave or otherwise my going to Delhi will not be that rewarding."

Latika sensed the seriousness of the matter. She switched off the gas burner and placed the pakoras on a tissue paper to drain out excess oil before transferring them on a plate. Meantime she poured tea in two cups and along with the plate of pakoras came out of the kitchen. She placed the tray on the table and sat down pulling a chair to hear more from Debjyoti who sat across the table.

"How did you find the girl?" Latika asked.

Debjyoti replied, "She was a victim of human trafficking. We took help of a Delhi based NGO that works for child trafficking cases as our NGO is not authorized for such case. Counseling the older girl gave us some vital clues. A team comprising the Delhi police, Assam police and the Delhi based NGO was formed to trace the missing girl. Luckily with the alertness of the Delhi police and the excellent network of the Delhi based NGO the girl was found during a raid operation in Seemapuri area. It was an excellent team work otherwise we could never trace the girl. Five more girls were rescued with her and sent back to their families. But Latika!" He turned to her," You are damn smart."

"What made you say that?"

"Your attempt of tracing the girl is not futile. Infact it was through the same lead we reached her. The difference is it took us twenty days and you took couple of days. Hats off to you mam! "

"He works with the NGO on human trafficking cases. I called you several times but there was no response. So I gave him all details unofficially."

"In fact we were amazed to find two teams from the same organisation tracing the same girl. In fact your guy was working unofficially yet his leads were concrete and showed results immediately. He was a member of the raid team and thus we came to know of him. He then told us about you being a friend whom he was helping out out of the way. You indeed did a good job."

Latika blushed. "Sachin elaborated me on the issue and I used my sources. Good that it helped you."

"It indeed did Latika. But the actual problem starts after the rescue. You see the problem lies in the source point from where these women and children are trafficked. After recovery the victims are back to the same poverty sticken families ending up in a vicious circle. They need proper rehabilitation so that they can make a difference to their family's economic condition."

"That indeed is a concern. In fact I was thinking of talking to you about this matter," added Latika.

"The new project that I have been assigned with deals with rehabilitation of these victims. I am going to Delhi for the training along with three more people from our organization. Let's see if we can really bring any difference in their life. So I am quite excited you see. I don't know how my organization is planning to start it but I think once we come back from the training it will involve lots of travelling for us to the sensitive areas. The best way to crush this trade is through awareness programs and proper education, unless we strengthen the economically weaker section of the society this crime will continue its pangs."

"It's a big job ahead then," Latika said.

"Yes and I need your support Latika," he said. "I cannot give in my hundred percent if at the back of mind I always have to think about your safety. So promise me you will always take care of yourself for me. "

Latika looked at him and answered teasingly," Why do you worry so much? "

Debjyoti thought for a while then answered, "Because I cannot afford to lose again Latika, it will break me completely and I have Kuki to look after too." He studied her for a while then said, "And if you don't then I will make you leave your work and force you to sit at home till I come back. And I mean it." Latika knew by the tone that he well meant what he just said. She promised him to take care of herself.

Debjyoti got up and went to the bedroom. He returned with a small gift box that he placed in front of her. He asked her to open it. She removed the wrapper and opened the box. It contained a small heart shaped pendent in gold.

"I picked it up for you in Delhi," he stated as he fumbled to open the latch of the gold chain hanging from his neck. He inserted the chain through the pendent and placed it around her neck. Then returning back to his seat he said,

"There it will always remind you of what you promised to me today."

Latika touched the pendent with her fingers that now rested in-between her breast close to her heart. She picked it up to her lips and kissed it.

"You are so unpredictable," she murmured.

"I am always prepared you see," he corrected.

"What if I had declined your proposal," she asked.

"You couldn't because you loved me," he replied. "Your eyes always spoke of your heart whereas your brain denied. When I met you in Shillong you were so much missing me that few days more together there you would have said it too."

Latika straightened herself in the chair hearing his statement. Every word he spoke was true but she didn't want to commit it. She said, "Yes because of the argument I had with you."

Debjyoti smiled hearing it. It amused him more to see her in defensive mode. He asked, "Do you remember missing anybody else so much after a heated argument, Latika?"

She knew he had had her there. She accepted her defeat saying, "None I can think of." Then she got up from her seat and planted a sweet kiss on his head. He pulled her down to sit on his lap and kissed her again as if he would never end.

Chapter Twenty Eight

Latika and her father spent that night at Snehlata's place. Next morning they set out with Shamsuddin to their home. The old man was pretty aware of the scene he would be witnessing in his neighborhood after the first shower of the monsoon. But Latika was taken for a surprise. She was terrorized to see the water logged areas of their neighborhood. The lanes were completely submerged under the overflowing ponds and open street drains. Water had seeped into many houses and people were either evacuating temporarily or were busy pumping off the water from their homes. The old man informed her that it was frequent scenes during rains as water from the nearby hills and high rising areas flooded the low lying areas of their locality. They got off from Shamsuddin's rickshaw and wadded through the ankle deep water to their home. Shamsuddin followed behind pulling his rickshaw.

Latika was in for a shock to see her premises after unlocking the gates. The courtyard bore a worn down look with branches of nearby trees and filth spread everywhere. Inside the house the entire flooring was smeared with muddy trails. Her father said that during heavy rains water from the courtyard seeped into the rooms and left behind the muddy trail after receeding.

Actually their house was situated in the foothills with several ponds surrounding it. And every time it rained heavily the water from these ponds overflowed and entered the nearby residential areas. Latika thought how hard it had been for her parents all the while but they never mentioned it to her. Actually she had never visited them during the monsoon. She started cleaning up the mess with Shamsuddin's help. Finally, after four hours of continuous sweeping and mopping the house was reinstated. Luckily it didn't rain till the afternoon that day and when it did it was not like the previous night. That gave a chance to the water level to receeded in several areas in the city. However, there were several low lying areas in the city that still faced the problem.

That day Latika didn't go to the office. Debjyoti had towed her car to the nearest garage as promised and before leaving for Shillong he had called her up. They chatted for a while then he hung up. Latika's father noted the sudden blushing of his daughter while taking the call but he didn't ask her anything. He wanted her to reveal it to him when she was ready. He was however pleased to see his daughter happy once more. That day they spent together cooking food and watching films on T.V. At night as it was still pouring Latika feared that water might seep into the rooms again. But her father told her that there was nothing to fear as it was not raining that heavily. However, the very thought disturbed Latika so much that she didn't want to sleep alone that night and made her bed in her father's room. Sleeping in their respective bed Latika asked her father about the flood problem in the area.

He said that when government had allotted this land for refugee rehabilitation it was a mere swampy area and people were dependent on the main city for all their day to day needs. The government had turned a blind eye to the community and even the basic amenities like water connection and hospitals were nowhere in the vicinity. However the community survived on its own and developed itself into an affordable area with time. The outsiders started relocating here to beat the cost of high living in the main city and thus the modern Kalapahar area took shape with numerous schools, offices, markets, restaurants and high rise buildings coming up. The overall development was unplanned and illegal with marshy areas filled up to make highrise apartments, drains covered to lay roads and hills cut down to build hotels. As a result water clogging turned out to be a major problem in the area. He pointed out to the grim situation of the Bharalu River which was reduced to a nullah now due to encroachment. Latika remembered the scene at the Bharalu River which she had come across during her slum visits. Although the residents were aware of the grime situation in the locality yet they turned a blind eye to the problem. Luckily it didn't rain heavily that night and Latika at last got some sleep.

But all was not well everywhere. People residing along the Bharalu River and the low lying areas of the slum were mostly affected while those in the elevated areas were untouched by the problem. Next day when Latika went to the office she found everybody busy with the relief operation. Volunteers were loading packets of biscuits, medicines, candles and bottled water in the hand carts. Even Shamsuddin was loading the relief material in his rickshaw. She went to Nayanmoni to ask him if she could also accompany them but he declined her offer. Instead she was assigned to procure more material from the Head Office. She hated it though but didn't say anything and worked silently.

****

Days passed and Debjyoti flew off to Delhi. Latika went to see him off at the airport. They didn't get much time to interact as he was with his team. With unspoken words he waved back at her as she stood at the entrance with her eyes trailing him till he disappeared inside. She returned home with a heavy heart that evening as for the next couple of months she could only contact him over phone and that too at his feasibility. She knew it would be a very long period of separation for both of them and they could do nothing about it. So she completely gave herself in to her work no matter how unchallenging it was. Nayanmoni, her new team leader, noticed the change in her and appreciated her efforts. He too knew she was yeaning to work with the others in the field but he didn't want to rush her to it as of now.

Meanwhile the rains continued on and off and news of several areas of the state reeling under grim flood situation topped the media. People were badly affected with their houses and property damaged. Many villages, agricultural lands were submerged under the flood water and life in several areas of the state was paralyzed. Several relief camps were opened throughout the state to help the victims. Some NGOs came forward to help the government agencies with the relief operations in these flood affected areas. Situation in Guwahati was also not very good with the Mighty Brahmaputra and its tributaries swollen up than their normal course. The city although under spell of monsoon showers continued with its normal life in spite of few areas affected due to water logging. In these areas schools and colleges were converted into temporary relief camps where people took refuge.

One such school in the Kalapahar area was also converted into a temporary relief camp where many people from the slum area had taken refuge. Latika's NGO provided relief material to the people in this camp. On one such occasion Shamsuddin had come to deliver the relief materials to the volunteers in the camp. He had taken couple of trips already and it was his last trip for the day. As he unloaded the material for distribution a young woman standing in the queue caught his attention.

Her fragile frame draped in a cheap printed cotton saree divulged the bulge of her pregnancy. She was desperately looking at the hands that were busy distributing the food packets to the people. Shamsuddin instantly felt a sting in his heart as he saw the woman. He was trying hard to see her face which was half covered by the veil of her saree.

The woman waited her turn impatiently for food packet and when she finally got one she ran inside the building. Shamsuddin followed her. She stopped in front of a room filled with people occupying space haphazardly. She made her way across the crowd to the far corner of the room where a man sat on the floor with a plastered leg and a child slept beside him. She removed her veil and opened the packet of food for him. Together they shared food from the packet.

Shamsuddin watched her from the corridor. Tears filled his eyes but he kept looking at her face till he could see no more. Slowly he wiped them off and looked at her again as if he would never stop. His little Adila has grown up in all these years. He was so surprised and happy to see her in front of him that he forgot to call her and talk to her. The moment was so tough for him that it frozed him to the ground. He could not utter a single word and just kept watching her from the open window. He left without approaching her.

****

Latika saw Shamsuddin walk into the office. He looked devastated. She quickly went to him and asked him what the matter was. Shyamhuddin could not control any further and broke down in front of her. He wept like a child wiping his tears with his *gamchha*. His whole world had come down finding his daughter in the temporary relief camp. Nothing was hidden about her pity condition from her appearance.

Latika tried to console him but he sobbed like a child. She had no idea what had happened to him. Between his sobs he uttered his daughter's name and wept. Latika stood by his side very much bewildered. Later when he regained his composure he told Latika his story. He told her everything about his family, how they disowned him till he met his elder daughter in the camp. When he was done he felt better, light at heart. He had known Latika long enough to confide to her. And his daughter's sudden appearance has disturbed him so much that he could think of only his Latika *Didi* for a shoulder to cry upon. Latika heard his story with patience. She didn't interrupt even once. She knew he must have gone through something terrible to reduce down to a state like this. Her heart ached hearing his story and she didn't know how to comfort him. In the end she suggested he should go and meet his daughter.

"No *Didi*, I don't want to meet her. It will be too much for me to hear the same words which my elder son had said to me. All these years I have consoled myself thinking that my children were getting a good life after Amina's decision. But today finding my daughter in this condition I am heartbroken, *Didi*. She was literally begging for food as if she had not had it for days. She looked so weak. I ….I..She was so beautiful and now…. That day they didn't give me a chance to talk to Adila and shut the door on my face. I tried several times to go back, *Didi* but could not." Shamsuddin was hysterical.

He continued. "I wonder why I had come to this city at all. I have lost my family, my house, my land everything since I came here. And now I have nothing to go back for. I should never have left my village and my family. What good did I make here? I am still struggling for survival. If you and *Mami* did not support me then I might have been dead by now."

"Please don't say that Shamsuddin. You have…."

He didn't hear Latika and continued. "They didn't mention the problems which a poor guy like me has to face in a big city life. Big Money dreams pull people like us from far off villages but how many of us actually survive here. And see! People are still coming here. What for? Somebody should stop them. Poverty stricken life in own village is much better than sleeping empty stomach on the pavement here. At least there are people to cry on your dead body. Here nobody cares for a soul like us. We are trash and our life is nothing but a stacked up trashbin that could never stop stinking even if empty." He wiped his eyes again and took out bundle of notes from his pocket that he had earned for the day.

"I have been saving money all the while for a house and get my family here oneday but see even today I am not in a position wherein I can ask my daughter to come and stay with me instead of the relief camp. I am a failure *Didi*, I still cannot support my daughter."

Latika understood his pain. She pulled a chair to sit across him. She said calmly, "Shamsuddin you are just thinking about yourself. You have never thought how happy your daughter might be to see you after so many years. I am a daughter myself and I can tell you that. And as you yourself mentioned that her husband has a fractured leg so in such a situation having somebody from the family can be the biggest support. I think you should go and meet her immediately. She might be in distress. And don't worry we will sort out something for you. "

Latika's statement puzzled Shamsuddin. He had never thought the other way like Latika. He looked at her confusingly. Latika repeated, "I am a daughter myself and I can tell you that." The statement injected confidence in the battered father and he rose to go and meet his daughter. Latika let out a sigh of relief and went back to her work. In her heart she earnestly prayed for Shamsuddin.

Chapter Twenty Nine

"Adila! My child," said Shamsuddin.

The young woman turned back and saw her father standing at the door. She could not believe her eyes. It had been such a long time since she last saw him. He looked much older yet had the same robust looks.

"Abba! Ya Allah! You are really here. I don't believe this. Abba...you.. " Adila could not complete as tears filled her eyes and her voice chocked. She ran to him and hugged him crying her heart out. Shamsuddin also could not stop himself as tears roll down his cheeks wetting his shirt. It was like home coming for both of them.

Adila introduced him to her husband who was watching them sitting on the floor and her three year old daughter who was playing nearby. Shamsuddin picked up the child in his lap and kissed her. Then took out a hundred rupee note from the folds of his lungi and handed it into the child's palm. The child got down and ran to her mother. Shamsuddin handed Adila the packet of food and sweets that he had brought for her. They chatted over the meal and later Adila sat on the stairs with her Abba for a heart to heart talk.

"Abba, I never thought of seeing you again and missed you so much. I was married off to another village and hardly ever got a chance to come and meet amma except on festivals. But that too minimized with years. My in-laws had a small cultivation land but with concurrent floods we lost it soon. My husband worked in a cycle repair shop and earned well to sustain the family. But Allah had some other plans for us. In the recent riots several houses in our village were torched down including ours. We were rendered homeless and penniless on the street for days but relief never reached us. I tried to go to amma's place but situation was tensed there too. Moreover my father in-law was not keeping well and died. We could do nothing about it. Finally we decided to move here to my sister-in-laws place. After all there was nothing to live for in the village anymore. My mother-in-law decided to stay back while we moved on. But Abba, nothing changed for us here too. He got a daily wager job with the contractor with his brother-in-law's help and I started working as a maid. Somehow we managed till the tragedy struck again and he fractured his leg. My family survived with my earnings alone as he could not work. But life came as a full circle when it rained and flooded our area. We were bound to leave the house and take refuge here. It's been a week since," said Adila with a sigh.

"Where is your sister-in-law?"

"They went to their village."

"What good is there for us here, Adila? We leave our village with a new hope but these big cities have nothing to offer for people like us. But you don't worry. With Allah's mercy your Abba is doing well here. So you don't have to worry anymore."

Adila smiled back at her father with tearful eye. She knew her father could never let them down anyways.

Later Shamsuddin came to know that his wife, Amina, had mothered two more children with her new companion and was leading a contended life. His children were going to school and were taken care of too. His heart ached to know that nobody in the family thought of him anymore. They had completely shut him out of their life and moved on whereas he was still there where they had abandoned him. Waiting for them to come back to him. Deep down his heart he knew he was given another chance and could not afford to fail this time. He felt a new strength within him with the only aim of resettling Adila and her family. Maybe it was the only way with which he could once again rejoin his family. And he thanked his Allah for it.

Next morning he sat down with Snehlata to calculate his savings that he had deposited with her over the years. He had to look for an accommodation for his daughter and her family to stay. He didn't want them to reside in the relief camp any longer. He told Snehlata about his daughter. She was happy for him but was sad too that he would be leaving soon. She considered him part of her family and promised to support him in all possible ways to settle down in his new place.

Shamsuddin hunted for an accommodation in the slum area. It was raining but that didn't stop him. He had promised Adila that he would shift her family from the temporary camp as soon as possible and he meant it. In so many years it was the first time he was looking for an accommodation for himself and it made him nervous. Earlier he had dreamt of owning a house but with his current savings that was not possible at this time. So a small rented accommodation was all he wanted at the moment.

The slum area was pathetic due to water logging in several places. But Shamsuddin kept knocking doors. It was late afternoon but no success. Failure started to dishearten him. Everywhere he went he was asked few questions first and then given the same answer. Tired of walking through the lanes he came upon the tea stall by the Bharalu River and sat down to rest for a while. He ordered for a cup of tea and some snacks. The overflowing Bharalu River across the dirt road caught his attention. The flood in the Bharalu had mercilessly driven off all the encroachment near it.

The old man handed the cup of tea and snacks to Shamsuddin and said, "Nothing will remain here in the coming years."

Shamsuddin was startled to hear the old man. The man continued, "When I came here this was a big river but now with so much encroachment it has been reduced to a *nullah*. But the day is not far when Bharalu will show its might and will eat up everything that comes its way. "

Shamsuddin hungrily munched on his snacks. Then taking a sip from the cup asked, "Why do you say so?"

The old man sat on the bench and looking at the overflowing river said, "Did you see the water current? It's eroding the banks every year. I use to catch fish once but there is none for the past few years. The water is poisonous with all sorts of waste materials being dumped into it. You must have seen the dark shallow water during the summers. Imagine the plight when this water enters our homes during rains. People are bound to get infection just by coming in contact with it."

The old man pointed towards the Miya patti and said, "That area was crowded with people just a few days back but today you see only water. I wonder how long my stall and house will survive."

Shamsuddin said, "*Chacha*, this side is little elevated so you don't have to worry for another ten years."

The old man laughed, "You bet that? If it rains for two continuous days the water will reach my stall. See! The erosion has already narrowed the dirt road. I and your *Chachi* are constantly in fear during rains."

He shifted his attention to Shamsuddin, "You tell me how you have been all the while. I have seen you after a long time."

"*Ho Chacha*! I have been little busy for sometime. I am looking for a rented accommodation."

"Did you succeed?"

Shamsuddin shook his head. "They don't even entertain a Miya Muslim here."

"They won't. You should look for in the Miyan patti."

"Half of the population of that area is residing in the relief camp *Chacha*. I doubt if I will get one."

"Yes it's a low lying area but you don't even have an option. At least you can try there. The other half of the population is still residing there at present."

"*Ho Chacha*! I will go there right away."

"I pray that you find one."

Shamsuddin paid the old man for the tea and snacks and left with a heavy heart. He reached the wodden bridge across the Bharalu that connected the Miyan patti to the main slum area. The water level was just few centimeters below the bridge. Something made him think hard and he retraced his path. He didn't go to the Miyan Patti that day.

The next few days he continued his searched in the *basti* only, but with no result. Either people did not entertain him because of his community or they had no accommodation to spare at the time. Samsuddin was growing weary day by day. The very feeling of failure gave him goose bumps. Every evening when he went to meet Adila, she waited with hopeful eyes but would be disheartened when he shook his head.

Days turned into weeks shortly and Shamsuddin had still not succeeded in his attempt. He was deliberately targeting accommodation in the elevated area of the *basti* so that his family would be safe even during rains and that part of the slum area mostly inhabited by the Non-Miyan community. But they didn't like Shamsuddin's presence in their area in the first place let alone rent an accommodation to him even if it was available. Still he didn't give up. At night he would wake up and think hard for the next day's visit. But with the passing time it was becoming difficult for Adila and her family to live in the camp. Their daughter was fallen sick due to drinking the contaminated water and there was no way Shamsuddin could see her suffer in the camp. So at last he crossed the wooden bridge across the Bharalu and reached the Miyan patti.

****

The scene churned his heart. The lanes were flooded with knee deep water out of the overflowing open drain in many places. Several houses had ankle deep water inside the premises as well. A foul smell of some decaying animal made it even terrible to breathe yet the occupants had no qualms about it. They were living inside with makeshift arrangements somehow.

Shamsuddin's stomach churned yet he waddled through the knee deep water into the colony with his lungee above his knees. The scene remained unchanged as he walked past the houses but he didn't stop. Eventually he reached Nafisa's house. Deep down Shamsuddin hoped of success at her doorstep. He knocked and waited rather impatiently. He had come here several times earlier yet it was the first time he knocked at the door.

Nafisa opened the door and saw Shamsuddin. She asked him to come inside without any second thoughts. He had helped her in many ways and she could never leave a chance to honour him. A smile of relief swept across Shamsuddin's lips as he followed her inside. It was the first time in all these days that someone almost a stranger had welcomed him with open arms. Nafisa offered him a glass of water and asked him about the reason of coming. Shamsuddin without any hesitation told her about the reason and earnestly hoped that she would help him.

Nafisa heard him then replied, "*Bhaijan*, you have already seen the scenario in this locality during rainy season. You should try after a month or so."

"What you say is true, *Apha*, but I cannot let my family live in relief camp anymore. I have to shift right away. I was thinking if you could help me."

"I will try *Bhaijan*, but it is quite difficult in this season as you can see. Let me see if I can do anything. Can you please come tomorrow?" she said.

Shamsuddin's face lit up hearing her. It was for the first time he heard someone giving him a positive reply since he started his hunt. He nodded and thanked her.

He slept peacefully that night and didn't go to meet Adila that evening. He wanted to finalize the accommodation first. He reached Nafisa's house late in the afternoon the next day. Her husband opened the door for him. Shamsuddin's heart raced as he waited for their reply. Both husband and wife didn't forget thank him again for his coordination in rescuing their nieces. Then they told him that they have come across an accommodation but it was very small and old. Shamshuddin could not ask for more. He nodded at them and set out to take a look at the accommodation along with them.

Chapter Thirty

It was an old single room accommodation near the bank of Bharalu River. The mud walls and tin sheet roof needed repair but luckily it stood alone on a slightly elevated area. So even though the lane was water logged the accomodation was pretty safe. A big smile swept on Shamsuddin's face as he thanked his Allah and the couple. Then they went to meet the landlord who lived in another lane to negotiate the rent. Shamsuddin agreed to his terms and gave him the token money.

He raced his rickshaw to the relief camp to break the news to Adila. She couldnot wait any longer and bundled her belongings to move to the new house with her family. No sooner had they reached home Adila sat down to clean it to make it more accommodable. She made up the cooking area and the sleeping area with the left over things by the previous occupant in the room. However there were still few things she needed to make a decent start but due to lack of money didn't utter a word. Shamsuddin saw her discomfort and reminded her again.

"You guys are my responsibility Adila. I am your Abba don't forget. So don't hesistate to ask for anything."

"I am sorry Abba. I didn't mean to hurt you. It's just that we don't want to burden you anymore," replied Adila.

"A child is never a burden on its father. You make me feel very small with that word. Whatelse I have other than you, my child?" snapped Shamsuddin.

Adila asked for forgiveness and quickly made a list of items she needed and told Shamsuddin. Shamsuddin happily bought the items and handed them over to Adila. Adila was once more busy with her work. She cooked meal while her husband, Azan, sat outside in the verandah with their daughter. Shamsuddin sat down beside him.

Azan looked at his father-in-law and said, "I don't know how to thank you Abba. Without you we would have been confined in the camp for Allah knows how long. You are a *Farishta* sent for us."

"Please don't say it, *Zamai*. I am just doing my duty. I have hardly done anything for any of them. Allah has given me a chance," replied Shamsuddin.

"*Ho* Abba. Had I not fractured my leg our situation would have been a little better and you wouldn't be burdened alone," said Azan sadly.

"We are family *Zamai* and being the head I have certain responsibilies. Till you are fine enough to look for work I will take care of you all. Even Adila need not work. She has to take care of you, Shaila and the unborn child. Once you start working then we can talk about sharing responsibilities. Till then let this ill fated father do something for the family," pleaded Shamsuddin.

Azan nodded. He thought for a moment and said.

"I want you to know something. When I married Adila I didn't know you were alive. We were told that you were missing and have always been an irresponsible parent. I always use to believe that but Adila always thought of you otherwise. When Shaila was born Adila didn't want her to hear anything bad about you so she stopped visiting her amma's place. I didn't interfere much but I asked her one day why she wasn't willing to visit her mother. Her answer still rings in my ears. She had said that how would I feel if Shaila spoke ill about me someday. I replied that I cannot live with it. She replied that she too didn't want to hear anything against her father which was quite obvious whenever she visits her amma's house. And therefore she had stopped visiting her mother. After that I didn't force her to go there. But my opinion about you hadn't changed until I met you. And today I am proud to admit that you are indeed a very responsible parent, Abba. Maybe circumstances were not in your favor at that time and people took advantage of it. But those were things of the past. We can make the present better."

Shamsuddin could not believe what he just heard. At least there was this one person, his daughter, who always had faith in him and by Allah's grace he was reunited with her. He remembered what Latika had told him about being a daughter.

Azan continued, "I have lost my *Babajaan* recently but I am glad that Allah sent you instead Abba."

Shamsuddin could not utter anything after hearing those words. His voice chocked in his throat and his eyes filled up with tears. He fought hard to push them back but a drop tickled down from the corner of the eye washing away the pain of betrayal that had fumed him for years. He quickly dabbed his *gamchha* into his eyes to prevent anybody from acknowledging his emotions.

Azan's wordings had breathed a new life in him. It was like he had seen light in the darkness. It was the moment he wanted to live forever. Later Adila served him home cooked meal with her own hands that he had missed for so long. At last he saw his long time wish of having meal with family in his own house, no matter rented one, was fulfilled. He was contended at last and remembered Allah for showing him mercy at last.

That evening Shamsuddin went back to Snehlata's place and finally took her leave. The old woman bid him farewell with teary eyes. He bent down and touched her feet and she blessed him. He collected all his belongings from the barn and promised to come to see her more often. Ten years had been a really long journey together for both of them. Several moments he had spent with his *Mami* sharing his grief and pain flashed past his eyes. He stood by the open gates and took a last look at the house that had nestled him so lovingly during his crisis. He gave a final wave to the old lady standing at the door from his rickshaw and rode off.

When he reached home after work all his tiredness vanished when Shaila came to snuggle him. It was another moment that he had been missing all these years. For few seconds he remembered the good old days in his village home. When he returned in the evening young Adila with her siblings would gather around him asking for sweet candies. He got a chance to relive his past in the new house with Adila's family.

At night Shamsuddin slept outside in the verandah while Adila and her family slept inside. Shamsuddin had insisted on sleeping outside as he knew it would be awkward for Adila and Azan to share a room with him at night. Though they kept on requesting him but Shamsuddin didn't listen. He didn't want them to have a strained married life because of him. And moreover he was quite used to sleeping outside. He cleared a small space in the verandah and made his bed. Then he hanged a plastic sheet at the end of the roof as a barrier to protect him from rain. All done he went to bed. The sound of Bharalu flowing below was quite audible at this part of the night. The humming sound of mosquitoes seemed like a lullaby and praising his Allah for all his greatness he went off to deep sleep.

****

Days passed into weeks and weeks into months. Shamsuddin lived every moment of his new found personal life with his daughter and her family. It didn't matter to him that all of a sudden he had so many mouths to feed and take care of that it was burning down his pocket and his savings. But he was very glad that whatever he earned was enough to sustain the family properly. Meanwhile Azan was also on the path to recovery and hoped to start working soon. After so much of struggle everything was going on fine in Shamsuddin's life and he never failed to thank Allah. He even took Adila and his granddaughter to the dargah where he had once taken refuge during his bad days. Adila had heard so much about Snehlata and Latika from Shaymshuddin that she insisted her Abba to take her to them too. Shamsuddin promised her when the time was appropriate he would take her to meet them.

Meanwhile Latika's life at work also came on track. She had been waiting to hear the news past so many months. She was very happy when Nayanmoni informed her that Deka, the main culprit, was nabbed from Jorhat. With him her *Sannyas* also came to an end. With all the culprits behind bars her road to social service opened once more.

Nayanmoni smiled at her excitement. "You can start from tomorrow if you want to," he informed her.

A smile swept on Latika's face. "Thank you," she answered and went out of the cabin. Her professional front had been completely dull since she started sitting in the office. Although the back office work was equally potential but Latika was more of an outdoor person and loved meeting people. She badly wanted to call up Debjyoti and break the news to him. However, she knew well enough that he won't be available at this hour to take her call. She had to wait till the evening. It had been almost two months now since he left for his training at Delhi and almost every other night they spent hours talking over the phone. Both were impatiently waiting for the day of his return.

The next day Nayanmoni clubbed her with Sachin for about week in the field. She was very excited. They left as usual with the team and started working in the slum area. Latika learnt his way of working gradually and remembered what Debjyoti had instructed her. This time she made sure she wasn't aggressive as before and worked more or less in a team.

In about a week she was ready to face the field on her own. She insisted to start her project from the same area where she had left earlier, the Miyan patti. Nayanmoni was little skeptical as he didn't want any incident with his team member again. But Latika was firm in her decision. Her logic eventually gave to Nayanmoni's nod. And she finally started her work in the area though much more consciously than before.

Shamsuddin was very happy to know her decision and accompanied her along with the team whenever needed. Her project initially started with a low response. But with Shamsuddin and Nafisa's help Latika spread word to mouth about how her NGO had saved the life of the two girls in the area. Her plan worked and the project managed to pull up good response from the people gradually. People who were initially not accepting her started respecting her work. The women folk who initially were skeptical now came forward to participate. Her work made her a known figure in the community and they easily approached her to share their problems. Latika too tried her best to help them and also educate them about health and hygiene which had always been Greek to them and the main cause of their several problems. She also never failed to keep her eyes open for any further incident of child trafficking. Latika unofficially started an awareness campaign about it too. She figured out that the problem lies in economic condtion of the people here. Being Miyan Muslims they were looked down upon by the society and were treated as illegal migrants. She came across many familes in the locality that have been living for generations yet were deprived of their basic rights. She planned an agenda to help them out in legalizing their identities with her NGO but the technicalities were way messier than she had thought it to be. Nevertheless she didn't lose hope and kept on her follow up.

Meanwhile she also started some vocational training programs along with some volunteers. She had visited the Head Office with her suggestions after scrutinizing the rehabilitation programs of the trafficked victims. She came to know that their NGO was not yet licensed for it. They have already started the procuring process and a team comprising Debjyoti and others were undergoing training for it. Latika hence started a service on her own at a very mico level along with few activists. Sachin was one of them. They targeted young girls and boys in the slum with any talent and helped them financially to undergo vocational training in the respective field which could help them to be financially independent. Their team mainly worked by finding new areas of opportunity for these slum children and placing them with proper training. With the NGO's tag behind them few of these children were readily accepted by the people as domestic workers, baby sitters, gardener and security guard.

The program although at a much smaller level received lots of appreciation both by the people of the NGOs and the slum community. Latika had once more proved her worth in the field. Nayanmoni was very much impressed by her work. Latika was so much involved in her work that she forgot the count of time. Days passed into weeks and weeks into months.

Chapter Thirty One

Like the rest of the country markets were decked up with all kinds of goodies to attract the customers with the onset of festive season. People were in festive mood be it Hindu or Muslim. Eid was round the corner and big pandals were already set up for Durga Puja celebration in many parts of the city. People were busy shopping for their family and home.

There was one more reason for Prachi to be happy. Her D Day was just a few days away and everyone in the office could see her excitement growing every day. She had made sure everyone in the office attended her wedding ceremony. Latika had her own reason to be happy. Debjyoti was returning back after completing his training in the coming week and he had planned to take a few days off before starting his new project. Nayanmoni was planning to go for a family vacation during the puja holidays while Sachin had his own plans. Everybody was counting days in the office. And so was Shamsuddin. He was going to celebrate Eid with family this year. He was already working hard to earn more money. He was also fasting in the holy month of Ramzan after many years.

One evening Latika was returning home from office in Shamsuddin's rickshaw. She broke into a conversation with him.

"Shamsuddin this year Eid will be very special for you."

"*Ho, Didi*. I cannot tell you how eagerly I am waiting for the day. It's been a long time since I actually celebrated it. Without family, life is nothing *Didi*."

"Yes, I agree. After ma's demise all the festivals seemed colorless but this year with *Pishi* it will be different. You must have heard that both of her sons are coming home with family during the puja holidays."

"Really? It is so good to know. *Mami* always misses them. Especially during the festivals! "

"Mothers are always like that. They never think beyond their children."

Latika's statement made Shamsuddin think about Amina. Surely she had chosen her children's welfare to him and it turned out to be a wise decision otherwise Adila would not have been married in time. He had butterflies in his stomach thinking about what the situation would have been otherwise. He already had five children to look after and had he lived with Amina maybe he would have fathered few more in matter of time. What sort of life could he possibly give them with his mere income? For a moment he was bound to think if his coming to Guwahati as a wise decision after all. Could he possibly succeed in providing them a better life had Amina not made her choice?

"What happened? What are you think of?"

Latika's voice brought him to realty. "I was scrutinizing the balance sheet of my life *Didi*. Back in the village my Abba left me a small piece of land but flood devastated it and I couldn't do anything about it. Since childhood I have been trying to meet the ends of the family. First, my father's family then my own but the situation did not change. Big city dreams attracted me too like the others in the village and I came here to make a difference to my life. But frankly *Didi*, if I look back I wonder what have I earned here. I have been working almost the same as in the village may be even more but my hands are as empty as ever. I doubt if anybody made it big after coming here. Moreover, I was wondering had I stayed back in the village how different my life would have been."

"It's human nature Shamsuddin. They say the grass is greener on the other side and we run only to find it pretty same as this side. The day we stop running maybe we could make a difference to our life."

"You speak so good, *Didi* that it makes me think sometimes."

Latika started laughing. "Don't worry. Thinking sometimes helps a lot."

"*Ho Didi!* If a poor man like me starts thinking how will be feed his family? We are born to work without using our mind and if we do, then it is a problem for us."

"No Shamsuddin. Thinking helps understanding things better. Hence it cannot be restricted to a particular class of

society. The level of thinking can be different but motive is all the same, to make things better. "

"That is true. What I had thought ten years ago before coming to Guwahati is not at all different then what my son-in-law had thought just few months back before coming here. The fact is even after so many years we are riding the same boat. Had I not helped them their situation would have been no better than mine with no work, no food and no shelter and no one to turn to at the time of crisis. Of course I have been fortunate enough to have *Mami* and you but everyone is not that lucky. All the dreams are shattered when crisis strike and you are left with possibly only two options. Either you run away or stick to the situation. But with people like me who have lost everything in the village there is hardly any option left. Where do we go, who do we turn to for help? I know Azan and Adila had no alternative when they decided to come here but situation here too has been the same for them. Who is there to listen to our woes *Didi*? And what's the point in thinking when nothing will ever change for people like us. We will keep on moving here from our villages for better life and meet our end in one of those stinky lanes one day. Unheard and unsaid. And nobody will even bother, Isn't it?? "

Latika was overwhelmed hearing him. He spoke his heart and every word of it was true. She had herself seen the living conditions of these people in the slum area and had never been able to do anything about it. Still the migration to bigger cities from the villages has never receded. In fact, every year the figure increases. As long as there is little scope of earning livelihood in the village level the figures in big cities will keep on increasing.

Latika could not make out what to say. She sat quietly as the rickshaw rode past the busy lane. When it finally pulled out in front of her house Latika took out a thousand rupee note from her purse and said, "Here is your Eidi Shamsuddin. Celebrate the festival nicely with your family."

He looked at the note in her hand longingly but denied taking. Latika insisted, "Please keep it. It's for your granddaughter. Buy something nice for her."

Shamsuddin took the money and smiled back at her. Latika smiled back and went inside the house. She found her aunt Snehlata sitting with her father.

"Oh what a surprise *Pishi*!" said Latika.

Snehlata smiled at her and said, "Yes dear. Today is a very special day you see."

Latika cried, "Oh God! Today is *Bapi's* birthday. I completely forgot. Please *Pishi* don't tell him. He... Oh God. What a stupid I have been."

"Don't worry dear. I have brought the cake. Now while your *Bapi* finishes his puja you can freshen up yourself then we can celebrate," said Snehlata. Latika sighed and gave a hug to her aunt.

Later they celebrated the old man's birthday and had dinner together. Since her uncle was out of town Latika insisted her aunt to stay the night. They slept in the same room and chatted till late. Over the conversation the old lady casually asked Latika about her life and if she had any plans to settle down in near future. Initially Latika hesitated but later on told her aunt about Debjyoti. She was thinking her aunt would be quite surprised to know about it but it was otherwise. She was quite cool. In fact Latika came to know from her aunt that her father already knew about her affair and was looking forward to meet him. Latika felt foolish hearing her aunt. All the while she had thought it was her little secret which she would reveal in proper time but little did she know that these oldies were much experienced in life and can easily count the feathers of a flying bird. She blushed and hid her face in the pillow and Snehlata laughed out loud.

Next morning over the tea Latika saw her aunt whispering something into her brother's ear and eventually both started smiling looking at her.

"Please *Bapi*. Stop making fun of me," pleaded Latika.

Her father replied, "We are happy for you, child. Don't get annoyed."

"I wanted to break the news to you, *Bapi* but you already knew it," complained Latika.

"Only a blind and deaf man cannot see your happiness, my dear. I am so happy for you. So when are you bringing him over to meet me?" asked her father.

"Very soon *Bapi*," she answered blushing again. Later she said, "But I want you to know something about him."

"What?"

"He is a widower and has a four year old daughter," saying she waited to see his response.

The old man adjusted his glasses and replied, "Yes I know that. Debjyoti had already told me about them and I have no problem with that. But Latika, have you thought about it? I just want you to be happy, child."

"Of course *Bapi* I am happy. But I have not met Kuki yet and her acceptance is far more important now," Latika answered. Her father and Snehlata nodded.

****

The plane landed and Latika saw Debjyoti coming out of the airport. She was eagerly waiting for him past half an hour. He waved his hand and taking leave from his team mates came running to her. Three months had been a long time for them and now it was their moment. They hurled in her car and sped towards the city.

The car halted in front of his apartment and they ran up the stairs like a sprinter in a hundred meters race. By the time they entered the flat both were panting. Debjyoti threw down his bag and hugged Latika without wasting a minute. She hugged him back with the same urgency. He kissed her wherever his lips traced and finally reached for her lips that were waiting long enough for his touch. Like a hungry animal he suckled her almost drawing her out of breathes. As she struggled for air he lightened his grip around her and started murmuring in her ear that sparked her ignited body even more for his touch. Her hands automatically burrowed into his shirt and started exploring his bare back that arched slightly wherever she touched him. He lowered his lips to her nape and rolled his tongue teasingly down her collar bone to her breast that he had cupped so lavishly. While with the other hand he fumbled inside through her tunic from the back and opened the clip of her bra. She moaned lightly in his ears as if telling him how much she had longed for it. Slowly he pulled down the tunic off her shoulder and cupped the naked breast like a priceless possession. She drowsily looked at him as he fondled it with one hand and his other hand at her back supporting her. Then he lowered his lips to the nipple and suckled. Latika arched back in his arms while he held him close to her. Then he reached for her lips while his other hand lifted her leg to his waist. She held him closer to herself as she felt his maleness thrusting deep down in between her legs. "Take me now," she whispered in his ears as he swept her off her feet into his arms and went inside the bedroom.

After their love making was over they lay quietly in each other's arms, naked. Debjyoti fondled with her hair as she rested her head on his chest. Time had stopped clicking for them as they remembered nothing accept each other's presence, the contentment of completeness clearly visible on their face as they rested peacefully in each other's arm. After facing the rougher side of life it was their moment now which they wanted to experience without any interference. But their moment was short lived as Debjyoti's phone buzzed and he got up to take the call. When he returned in the room his expression was different.

"It was Kuki. I have to go Latika. She is waiting for me," said Debjyoti as he sat on the bed beside her naked body.

"Are you leaving now?" she asked.

"Maybe an hour or so," he replied. "Why don't you come along?"

"Me?? What will I say to *Bapi*?"

"Tell him you are going with me."

"That's not possible, you know it."

"But how will I stay there without you? And I cannot even leave Kuki. The poor child is waiting for me." he said sadly. "In these three months only god knows how crazily I had missed you. I am obsessed with you and look at you. How coolly you are saying you can't." He was complaining like a child.

Latika sat up and pecked a sweet kiss on his cheek. "Even I missed you badly. Look at me. Can't you read in my eyes," she said.

He looked at her rather confusingly. "I don't know. I want you too to come along. Please do something" He insisted.

Latika thought about it then said, "Why don't you bring her here? It will give me a chance to meet her as well as we can spend some time together."

"Here? I have never handled her alone. She is too small and I don't know if I can take good care of her here," he said.

"Of course you can. No matter how small she is but you are her father. And every father has an instinct of knowing the needs and wants of his child. You yourself said she misses you badly. So if you bring her here you two will get a lot of time to spend together and moreover I shall be there to help too. "

Debjyoti thought over her suggestion. It seemed good one. He gave his nod to it and felt relieved. Once his tension subsided he regained his old self and indulged in love making once more and they spent time together till it was time to catch the bus to Shillong.

Chapter Thirty Two

"Shamsuddin you look very happy today! Whats the news?" asked Snehlata from the kitchen.

"*Mami*, Azan's plaster has been taken off today. The doctor said he can start working in few days," replied Shamsuddin happily.

"Oh! That's really good news. So when are you bringing your family to meet me?" asked Snehlata.

"Adila will take a while to come here. As you know she is expecting anytime. But I will bring Shaila. She talks about you the whole day," replied Shamsuddin.

"Yes I have her Eidi ready but I shall give it in her hand. And wait I have something for you too." Snehlata went inside the living quarter and brought a packet. She handed it to Shamsuddin.

"Here I have bought something for all of you. I hope you will like it."

Shamsuddin looked inside the packet. It had a beautiful saree, two set of pyjama kurta and a cute frock.

"*Mami* you give me something every Eid and now for the whole family? I don't know what to say. Actually this time I got something for you. Durga Puja is round the corner and I know you will buy something for your house. Here please accept it." He undid few buttons of his shirt and took out a small packet wrapped in paper. He placed it carefully in her hands.

Snehlata opened the folds of the paper and saw a beautiful hand embroidered bedcover. "Wow! It's beautiful."

"Adila did the embroidery stitches. Though she stitched it long time back before coming here. She kept it with her as a precious possession all these years," said Shamsuddin. "She wants you to keep it as a token of love."

"Its lovely. Tell her I loved it. She has such fine hands on stitching. Should always keep it up," claimed Snehlata.

"*Ho Mami*. If things go out fine then in near future I will get her a sewing machine. She can work from home," said Shamsuddin.

"You can take my sewing machine right away. It is lying unused for years."

"Thank you *Mami* but no. I will buy her one myself. All these years I could not do anything for any of my children. But now I have something to live for and I shall help them in all possible ways. It's so nice of you to consider it *Mami*. Thank you once again."

They chatted for some time more over cup of usual red tea and biscuits then went on with their work. Snehlata thought of the change in Shamsuddin. All of a sudden he was filled up with spirit of life which she had never seen before. She liked his self confidence and prayed for him.

****

Latika was nervous like never before. She was going to meet Kuki finally. It had been three days since Debjyoti was back from Shillong with his daughter but Latika could not go to meet them. She wanted the duo to spend time with each other till she made an appearance. And today the day had come when she was finally meeting the little girl. With Debjyoti's suggestion she draped a sari and stepped out of the house nervously. She knew at heart that the child's acceptance is very important for their relationship.

She sighed and rang the door bell of his flat. Her heart was racing so fast that she could hear it loud enough. She feared that others might hear it too. Since previous night her hands and feets were cold with the thought of getting interviewed by Kuki. Though she was too small yet she had a big say in Debjyoti's life. Debjyoti had already told her that back home he had left no stone unturned in promoting her in front of Kuki but he also alerted her that the child was the ultimate authority for their future as the lady in his life has to be accepted as the mother first and then his wife.

Latika religiously followed all the advices Debjyoti had given her for this meeting. He particularly insisted that she should wear a saree and a bindi on the forehead rather than her jeans and kurtis. The advice had taken Latika a complete two hours to get the getup as she was not use to draping the six yards much and before that two hours more to decide on.

At last she had called up her aunt and narrated her dilemma to the old lady.

"Latika you are either expecting too much or may be thinking too much. Don't confuse yourself. Why do you think you are going to meet Debjyoti's daughter? Rather go and meet a four year old child. I am sure she will be fun to have around. Just be your self!"

The old lady's wordings did some kind of magic to Latika and she was ready within minutes. Surely Debjyoti had injected his own fears in her all the while but she had shrugged him off and set out with new found confidence.

Waiting outside the door, suddenly she felt she was reliving some moment in the past.

"A sweet dream that evoked the feeling of need in her, need of companionship, feeling of being in love, a feeling of longingness. She only had a vague memory of opening the door for someone."

A blend of excitement and nervousness gripped her. She heard someone struggling with the door latch behind and finally it opened for her. Her heart skipped a little for what she saw.

Right in front of her was a smaller version of Debjyoti looking straight into her eyes. She stood on a stool by the side of the door with an ear to ear smile saying, "Hello, Latika aunty."

Latika could not help smiling. All her nervousness vanished as she looked into those innocent eyes of the smiling child. "Hello, Kuki," she replied and helped the child to get down from the stool.

Kuki ran inside calling her father, "Papa! Papa! See who has come?" A little later she reappeared saying, "Papa is in the shower."

"It's O.k. I came to meet you," said Latika making herself comfortable in the chair.

The child thought for a while and replied, "But you are Papa's friend. Why should you meet me?"

Latika understood the sensitivity of the question and replied, "Because you are Papa's best friend and I want to be friends with you too."

"But you are so big. You don't play with dolls anymore?"

"I do! I have two big dolls to play with."

"Did you bring them?"

"Oh! I forgot. But I have something for you." Latika dug in her hand bag and took out a small teddy bear. "This is Chiki and he wants to be friends with you too."

Kuki looked at the soft toy in her hand and grabbed it. "I shall be friends with Chikki," she replied and cuddled the toy in her hand. She came over and sat down beside Latika then said, "Latika Aunty! You look so different than the picture Papa showed me."

"What picture, dear?"

Kuki ran inside to bring Debjyoti's cellphone. Latika was very impressed by the child's smartness in handling the phone as she showed her the picture. It was one that they clicked in the office party.

"Yeah that's me. But how do I look different?"

Pat came the reply from Kuki, "You are more beautiful than the picture."

Latika laughed out. She could easily make out that the child had noticed the difference with the saree. "You like it?" she asked.

"I love sarees. Can you drape me one." Kuki asked innocently.

"Sure. Why not? I will get you a saree for Durga Puja," replied Latika. Kuki nodded.

By the time Debjyoti came to join them Kuki had already discussed all her interest and disinterest with Latika. She hated Maths and loved to dress up like "Kusum" of the daily telesoap. Debjyoti was very happy to see both the girls engrossed in hot discussion.

The trio passed a wonderful time together that day. In short time Kuki grew so fond of Latika that when it was time to say goodbye the child insisted that she come back again the next day. Latika promised and came back again the following evening. Eventually she started spending more time with Kuki.

They went to the mall, amusement park, zoo, movies and even did the Durga Puja shopping together. With every passing day Kuki's demands kept increasing Kuki. She wanted Latika to be around her most of the time. Other than fun she wanted Latika to feed her, dress her up, bathe her and much more. She even wanted her Latika Aunty to stay over the night too. Kuki's demands were so innocent that it pained Latika to break the child's heart sometimes but she had no option left.

Debjyoti was very amazed to see his daughter. Latika's presence had somehow nullified the gap of a motherly figure in Kuki's life in such a short span of time that Debjyoti was not aware that his daughter missed a motherly presence so much. Latika fitted in the bill perfectly. Now he had no qualms in going to meet Latika's father.

Two days later he met Latika's father over dinner and asked for the old man's permission to marry his daughter. Latika's father gave his approval without any second thoughts.

Few days later Latika and her father headed for Shillong to meet Debjyoti's parents. His mother was Khasi while his father was Assamese. It was a formal get together of the two families and they eventually approved the wedding of the duo. Two days later ring exchange ceremony was held in Debjyoti's uncle's guest house which was attendended by Latika's aunt and uncle from Guwahati and some close family members from Debjyoti's side.

In the whole event it was Kuki who grabbed the eyeballs. She looked the happiest of all and didn't leave Latika's side even for a second in the entire event. Debjyoti's mother was overwhelmed to see her grand daughter's behaviour. She called Latika aside to thank her for willing to take care of the two people she adored most in the world. Latika hugged her.

Chapter Thirty Three

As the days passed the festival fever gripped the people even more. Guwahati city was no different than the rest of the country. Markets and shops were flooded with people for the last minute shopping. People either did it for Eid celebrations or for Durga Puja as both the festivals were scheduled back to back. It was a time when people didn't mind spending money. It was also the time of family reunion. People started taking leave from work to go to their home town to celebrate the festivals with their family. Several offices were completing their pending work before closing down for puja holidays.

As the Muslims of the city decked up for Eid celebration so did the Hindus for the Durga Puja. The latter being a big festival of the Hindus of the state and was celebrated with great pomp and show. Huge community pandals or temporary temples with latest themes and decorations were set up at every nook and corner of the city. The pandal decoration and theme always remains a major attraction during the puja. Added to it were the life size idols of the deities in these pandals.. People, dressed in their best new attire, indulged in pandal hopping activity during the puja festival. Community feast and cultural programs were the other main attractions of these pandals. People with their familes and friends thronged these pandals from morning till late night.

Snehlata's two sons had also come home with their families and the usually gloomy house bloomed up once again with the laughter of children and family members. Snehlata was never so busy and happy before. She was having a tremendous time with her grandchildren who were much grown up since their last visit. Latika was too excited as after a long time she was going to celebrate the festival in her native place.

Latika and her father came to visit Snehlata. Since her engagement she couldnot take out time to meet her aunt. She was very thrilled to meet her cousins and their wives. She had a gala time with her sister-in-laws. They exchanged gifts and made plans for the evening while making delicacies in the kitchen. They still had some last minute shopping at hand and planned to go to the market in the afternoon. Snehlata too gave off presents to everybody in the family on occasion of the festival. The situation was more or less the same in almost every house. And it was no different in Shamsuddin's house. He too had done Eid shopping for everybody in the family. He knew the day would be special because of his family. For the first time in so many years he was spending money on his family on the occasion of Eid.

****

Finally it was Eid. The Muslim dominated areas of the city bore a festive look since the past couple of days. The lanes were decorated with banners and flashy lights. The men folk dressed in their traditional attire thronged the mosque and open areas for offering their morning prayers. Children dressed in their new clothes added to the celebrations in the household. The homes were equally decorated for the celebrations. The women folk too looked their best for the occasion with their new clothes and jewelry. People went to meet each other exchanging Eid greetings with his friends and relatives. Evenings were even more special with feast round every corner of the lane where families and friends gathered to have a blast on the auspicious occasion.

The Miyan patti too bore a festive look with numerous flashy lights and banners adorning the lanes. People were busy meeting each other and exchanging Eid greetings. The day had been very special to Shamsuddin. He had a family now. Azan and Adila had given a new meaning to his life which was otherwise just lingering on. Since morning he had been busy offering his prayers and meeting his friends. In the evening he took Shaila to the feast which the child enjoyed a lot. Adila had prepared "Shemai" and several other delicacies that reminded him of Amina. Every bite he took touched his heart.

Late at night when Shamsuddin finally went to sleep in the verandah outside he could not hold back his tears. He thanked his Almighty once more for showing mercy. From where Shamsuddin slept he could clearly see the lane to his house. The flashy lights illuminated the whole lane. There were still numerous people hustling and bustling in the lane. He watched them for sometime then turned sideways.

The Bharalu flowing beneath caught his attention. With the rains off for some time the once swollen river was reduced to a "*nullah*" once more carrying down the city waste into the River Brahmaputra at a much slower pace. The reflection of the flashy lights of the lane amazingly glittered in the flowing water of the river. The lights danced on the ripples while the tinkling sound of the water flowing along with crickets chirping nearby added ambiance to the visual affect. Shamsuddin enjoyed it for some moments then went off to sleep to a lovely dream, a dream that he more often saw nowadays. Slowly all the nearby sounds faded off as he dozed off completely.

The Bharalu and its tributaries played a major role as the natural drainage system of the city but as human beings have the tendency to take everything for granted this river was also not spared. With several illegal encroachments along its embankment and irresponsible dumping of waste into its water the natural flow of the river was badly affected and so was the river bed. The affects of its negligence was clearly visible during the monsoons when with the slightest downpour the river swells completely posing a big threat to the localities in its vicinity.

The authorities of the water resource department and the flood control department were not totally unaware of the situation. Time and again they worked out strategies and informed the concerned department about the necessary steps required to be taken for the upkeep of this natural resource but the action would always take its due course to be excecuted.

It was a similar situation that night too when the city finally went off to sleep after celebrating Eid. The man on duty at the sluice gate station in Bharalumukh, the meeting point of Bharalu and Bhramputra River, took notice of something faulty and immediately informed the authorities. The next morning the team of maintainence staff conducted the survey and did the necessary repair works to their satisfaction. It was a minor repair work but it did call for a strict vigilance by the concerned department. However, with the Durga Puja festival round the corner most of the people were with a laid back attitude at work and thus the vigilance was vaguely done.

****

It was the first day of the puja celebration. Several offices including Latika's had closed down for puja holidays. People thronged the pandals from morning till late night. Dressed up in their new attire people hopped around from one pandal to another with their families and friends till late night. Motor vehicles were restricted in several areas during the festival days for easy commutation of the crowd to the pandals. This gave chance for people like Shamsuddin to make good money ferrying people to the pandals. Like Shamsuddin the roadside food stalls owners too earned few bucks by offering snacks and drinks to the passer by. The festival generated business for almost everybody and people were so much engrossed in its celebration that no news bothered them anymore.

The met department predicted heavy downpours in the hilly areas of neighboring Arunachal Pradesh in the next few days. The authorities of the state were having sleepless nights getting the news. It implied flood situation in the lowlying districts of the Assam state. The situation was not new to them. The state witnessed flood twice or thrice every year during monsoons. The departments were ready to take the challenge while the people enjoyed the moments of the festival.

It started drizzling the next morning and continued till the whole day. But people went on with their life as usual. By evening drizzling stopped and some of the city roads were water logged. But that didn't stop the crowd from rushing to the pandals. Even in knee deep water in some areas people went to enjoy the festival. With just a few accusations to the governing bodies they went on with their celebration till the last day irrespective of the rains that were on and off.

Finally the day arrived when the deities were bidden goodbye with tearful eyes amid much pomp but the festive fever was still on and people were still basking in its ambiance unaware or least bothered of the situation in the state. Flood had now been a part of life of the people of the city so they did not wither away anymore. They continued with their festive fever without any disruption.

Meanwhile, the heavy downpour in Arunachal Pradesh caused flood in the adjoining lowlying areas of Assam state as predicted earlier. Many districts were affected by floods causing heavy damage to the lives and properties of the people. The Assam State Disaster Management Authority had already started the relief operations in these areas full fledgedly and announced a red alert in Guwahati city as well. Luckily the city didn't witness any rainfall further. The sky was clear and the water level in the Bharalu River and its tributaries that ran within the city were normal. However the Brahmaputra River in Guwahati showed an alarming increase in its water level.

The sluice gates at various intersections within the city were closed to avoid reversal of flood water from Brahmaputra to Bharalu and its tributaries. But Brahmaputra was showing no sign of mercy. Its water level had long crossed the danger mark within few hours and was rising inch by inch with each hour passing by posing a big threat to city. With it's pace the water could submerge the entire city of Guwahati and Dispur within a short span of time. People gathered around the road along the riverside to see the mad fury of Brahmaputra while praying to "Ma Kamakhya", the sacred goddess of the city, for their safety.

Chapter Thirty Four

People let a sigh of relief when at last their prayers were answered. The water level in the Brahmaputra minimized further escalation. However the threat was still not over untill the water level receeded. That night probably no one blinked an eye. Everyone in the city was on alert. The news channels updated about the situation every now and then. Finally the water levels showed a marginal descend by dawn. For people of the city the sign was enough to predict the danger had subsided. Smile swept on every lip and hands folded together again in conveying "Thanks" to "Ma Kamakhya." It had been a really long day that ended on a positive note. Sleep was inevitable.

Shamsuddin hit his pillow and was in dreams in no time. The week had been too hectic for him. Firstly due to Durga Puja and then the Brahmaputra threat. The later had really been very spine chilling for him. He had already experienced the fury of flood back in his village and the nightmares haunted him for several years. Guwahati was considered much safer than his village but the previous day's situation didn't fail to give him goose bumps.

A sudden tremor woke him up late at night. It wasn't unusual in Guwahati. The city resting on active seismic zone experienced such tremors more often. It lasted for just few seconds only and didn't call for any attention. Though Shamsuddin lay wide awake. The pale light of the half moon in the sky illuminated the nearby contours. It was peaceful around other than the running water of the Bharalu below and the crickets chirping. He thought of relieving himself first before going to sleep again. He got up from his bed and moved towards the bushes in the far end of the house.

A few kilometers down the Bharalu at the Bharalumukh, the sudden tremor had its affected on the closed sluice gate. The repair work gave way and before anything could be understood the flood water from Brahmaputra came gushing into the Bharalu flooding it in no time. From the Bharalumukh intersection till the other end Bharalu suddenly came alive as the flood water reversed back its course bloating it up in no time and ravishing everything that came in its path.

Shamsuddin was almost done when the gushing down of water in the Bharalu below caught his attention. He turned back and saw Bharalu. It was a spine chilling sight as the dirty gushing water came charging at an alarming speed. With the blink of an eye the water flooded the embarkment and washed away everything in its way. Before Shamsuddin could realize anything he saw the earth beneath his house caved in collapsing the old structure along with it into the gushing water. His family, who had been sleeping inside, drowned with it in front of his eyes. He tried to shout but found himself in neck deep water that dragged him along in its flow. With some efforts he somehow managed to grab hold of something strong and pull himself up from the water. Wherever his eyes went he saw only water and cries of people. He blacked out.

****

It was 2.00 a.m in the morning and Kalapahar woke up to the cries of people. People didn't know what was going on. There was no electricity and all they heard were the cries of women, children and men for help. Stampede of people running across the roads towards the uphill area shouting for help.

Latika too woke up hearing the cries. She switched on her night lamp but there was no electricity. She stepped down from her bed and landed into knee deep water socking her pyjamas. Terrified she reached for the torch on the night table and switched it on. She was traumatised to find her room flooded. The water level almost reached her bed wetting the mattress. She didn't waste time and wadded through the water to check upon her father's room. It was similar situation there too with only difference that the old man was sound asleep due to medication. She woke him up and went to check the other rooms.

It was similar sight all around. Dining chairs, gas cylinder, utensils, tables everything floating across the rooms. She switched off all the switches and whatever valuables she could laid her hand upon she collected in a bag. Then she pulled a chair on top of her father's bed and made the old man sit on it with the bag. She checked the water level outside through the glass window with the hope of evacuating the house. But it was worse and more risky to wander out with an old man in flood water at night. She knew she could not make it.

Help was unreachable as of now as everyone was fending for themselves. She heard the neighbors crying for help but no one listened. Even the cell phone network was jammed. She knew she could not do anything but wait. At last she pulled a chair on the bed and sat down beside her father clenching his hands in hers. Both prayed eagerly for all this to be over.

****

Meanwhile the men at the Bharalumukh station managed to restore sluice gates manually and check the reverse flow yet the damage was done. The encroachments along the embankment of Bharalu were washed away completely and the lowlying areas in its vicinity were under waist deep water.

Although the water level showed a remarkable stability within an hour yet it showed no sign of receeding. That night was the longest night ever when the people witnessed the fury of Bharalu. The casualty was more as it was late at night and people were sleeping. Most affected were the children, sick and old. They could not resist the force of the water and were washed away. People were running for help. It was sheer chaos everywhere.

By dawn the first help arrived. The locals rushed out to help the victims. Several areas in the slum had waist deep water. The most effected was the Miyan patti where the water was neck deep. The connecting wooden bridge was already submerged which made it difficult for the locals to help the people on the other side.

Till then nobody knew how it had happened or how much destruction was caused. People had taken refuge in the stadium and nearby school buildings or in their relative's house. The scene was very pathetic. Those affected were still in shock and locals helped them in whatever ways possible. By morning the swollen Bharulu River had started receeding and leaving behind a trail of devastation.

Latika too managed to reach Snehlata's house with her father with the help of some locals. Luckily her aunt's house being near the foothills remained untouched by the devastation. Latika and her father were in deep shock. Snehlata and her husband did everything possible to make them comfortable. That day Latika slept throughout the day after taking medication.

****

The whole day the news updated about the whole situation. The Kalapahar area being densely populated along the Bharalu was the most affected. The locals and the administration came to rescue the victims. What remained behind needed to be reinstated. Wounded were admitted to hospitals and the loss calculated. The locals and administration offered help in all possible ways. The relief camps were visited by all sorts of officials to figure out the actual loss throughout the day. Nayanmoni and his team too came to help in the relief operation since the morning. They learnt about Latika's whereabout but didn't disturb her.

People helped the survivors reunite with their families. However not everybody was that lucky. It was a pathetic sight to see mothers weeping for the loss of their childen and children weeping for loss of their family members. There was nothing that could compensate this loss. Shamsuddin was one of them.

He was lucky enough to have survived but the loss was unbearable for him too. In front of his eyes he had witnessed Adila and her family washed away when the house caved in. He had little doubts about their survival. Nevertheless he rested his faith in Allah. Although he was not hurt much physically yet emotionally he was dead. He was still in shock when the rescuers brought him to the relief camp. With little first aid he was let go. But nobody could forsee his mental situation.

Whole day he looked for his daughter and her family in all possible areas but found no trace of them. By evening his little hope too vanished. Several bodies were recovered from the site and handed over to the families for the last rites but Shamsuddin didn't had any more courage left within to look for his family there. He returned back to the relief camp and sat down in a corner. Beside him sat a family wailing the loss of their family member but Shamsuddin sat lost in his own thoughts unaware of everything around him.

Next day Latika too set out with her team to help people in the camp. Her house was not her priority at this time. Her father was well taken care of at her aunt's place and she focused on the needy victims in the relief camp who needed more assistance immediately. She worked with the team the whole day in the camp and by evening located Shamsuddin in one of the camp. He sat aloof from everybody else in one of the rooms full of people. It took Latika sometime to recognize him with his beard and torn dirty clothes. He looked starved and sick while his eyes wore a blank look. He did not respond when latika called him. She tapped him twice before he looked at her. There was no sign of recognition in his eyes.

"Shamsuddin I am Latika *Didi*. Didn't you recognize me?" Latika said sadly. But Shamsuddin didn't reply and turned his face off her.

She asked again, "Where is Adila and others?" But Shamsuddin seemed too distant to hear her. His eyes bore the same blank look as if he belonged to a different world.

Latika's heart cried out to see him in this condition. She checked out with the camp authorities and found out that he had filed a missing complaint for his daughter and her family. But so far there was no information about them. She informed Nayanmoni and Sachin about Shamsuddin's condition and they immediately took the charge of the matter. Meanwhile Latika admitted him in the hospital. She could not bear to leave him in the camp unattended. She was quite at ease after leaving him under the doctor's care. She had done what she could for him and prayed to the Lord for his recovery.

That night she didn't sleep nor did Snehlata. When Latika told her about Shamsuddin the lady broke down to tears. Ten years he had spent in her barn sharing her gloominess with a smile on his face. But when he set out for the better, everything that he ever accumulated scattered in split of a second. Both the ladies thought of him and blamed themselves for knowing so less about him. At the time of need they knew no one from Shamsuddin's family whom they could inform about his condition. They had never met Adila or anybody else in his family. And now there was no clue of them too.

Early next morning both of them went to meet Shamsuddin in the hospital. The doctor informed them about his detoriating condition. Latika knew that it was about time when his family members had to be informed about his condition. Though she remembered Shamsuddin telling her about his family's betrayal yet she believed a dying man's last wish should be fulfilled. The brief time she had known Shamsuddin he seemed as a very family loving man and it was only love for his family that made him survive against all odds in Guwahati. Latika knew she had a big challenge.

****

The government announced compensation and rehabilitation plans for the victims of the flash flood. Latika was happy that at least there was something Shamsuddin or his family could bank upon. But it came as a big surprise for her when she got in touch with the administration.

Since the majorities of the victims belonged to unauthorized colonies along the Bharalu the loss was majorly minimized on official papers. The Miyan patti area was one such unauthorized colony considered to be inhabitated by the "illegal migrants or Bangladeshis". So none of the victim existed on the government papers and hence was not eligible for any government compensation and rehabilitation. The only aid they got was the clothing and food supplies in the relief camp and that too were entitled to it till the camp lasted. After which they had to fend for themselves.

Government aid was limited to the victims of legitimate colonies only.

The information came as a big blow to Latika. Till now she had only heard about the term, "illegal migrants" but here she was witness to the fact as how people like Shamsuddin got affected. There was no way to decipher this segment of people from the actual "illegal migrants" who were the main culprits. People like Shamsuddin being poor and illiterate had always bore the bruise without any fight and will continue to do so till they know about their rights. There was nothing Latika could do about it but it disturbed her to the depth.

Meanwhile Latika's search for Shamsuddin's family too came to a dead end. Neither could she trace his daughter and her family nor did anybody have any information about them. People in the camp were too occupied with their own miseries to help her out yet she kept on with her search and accidently tumbled upon Geeta who once had a relationship with Shamsuddin. Geeta gave her some vital information about Shamsuddin's village.

Latika took her NGO's help in reaching Shamsuddin's family in Barpeta. A volunteer from their nodal office in Barpeta went to visit Shamsuddin's family in the village but as luck had its toll the guy gave the message to Fakrru instead of Amina who in turn denied having any links with the dying man. When Latika came to know about it she was very disheartenend. Her heart ached to know that his family didn't care about a dying man. Snehlata was more grieved hearing about it from Latika. Both Latika and Snehlata felt sorry for him.

"He is not without family. I am his family. What if the customs and community forbid me to do anything for him but at heart he has always been a son to me. Tell him his mother is here to take care of him. I shall do whatever it takes to make him happy," said Snehlata.

The next day both of them went to visit Shamsuddin again and tried all means to convey him that they really wanted him to pull through. But Shamsuddin didn't show any response. He lay still in his bed looking vaguely towards the ceiling with the same blank look in his eyes. The doctor briefed them that if he did not respond soon then it will be fatal for him.

Shamsuddin's condition further deteriorated in the next two days. He stopped taking food completely and didn't respond to any medication anymore. That night he breathed his last.

Chapter Thirty Five

Shamsuddin saw his own body lying in the hospital bed, weak and lifeless. It bore no resemblance to what he was used to seeing in the mirror, a strong, lively man full of energy. On the bed below lay a shrunken, lifeless body that he could not recognize. He started weeping but the doctors and nurses standing near the bed were taking no notice of him. They were busy doing their duty with the patient's body before shifting it out of the ward. It never appeared to Shamsuddin that after death he was nothing more than a spirit and what lay beneath the white sheet on the hospital bed was his dead body.

His spirit was trying hard to draw attention of the attending doctor and nurse but it was useless. They showed no sign of acceptance of its existence. It took him sometime to realize that he was no more what he used to be. It felt like something heavy and worn out had been taken off him and replaced with something translucent and as light as feather. It felt just like the wind which could neither be heard nor seen but very much existed. He soon realized that he was dead. He wept over his dead body and tried to stop the ward boys from taking the body out of the ward. But it was of no use. In the end he quietly followed his body to the morgue.

Waiting beside his body in the morgue he slowly recalled everything. He didn't know how he reached the hospital. He only remembered the house had caved in drowning Adila and others in the gushing water. He remembered clinging on to something strong before blacking out. So at least he did not die of drowning. But surprisingly he remembered nothing after that and wondered what happened to him. How did he reach the hospital? His eyes moistened thinking of his own death. Thirty five years of his life and he earned nothing. Not a single person cared when he was alive and now his death would hardly have any grievance by anybody.

His Allah had been too "picky" on him. Since childhood he had been suffering at the hands of his fate. Poverty and ill fate had always been on his side as long as he lived. No matter how hard he tried he was always back to square one. After meeting Adila he had thought his life might change a little but it was again back to square one. He was as alone as ever. He made sure that when he met his Allah in the heaven he would surely raise the issue. He had dutifully offed his prayers throughout his life yet Allah had forsaken him. Indeed he had a lot to settle with his Allah.

Latika's arrival in the morgue interrupted his thoughts. He never thought she would be here. He had no clue how she came to know about him and what was she doing here at this time of night?

Latika came over to the body and lifted the sheet. Tears rolled down her eyes. She watched the lifeless body for few minutes and called up Snehlata. Just then the doctor came up to her and briefed her about the hospital proceedings of handing over the body. In the end the doctor praised Latika for her selfless service in helping out people like Shamsuddin. He was especially impressed by Snehlata who beared all the expenses for the treatment. He expressed his gratitude in being of any help for such a noble cause.

Latika heard every word the doctor said with tearful eyes. She did not hesitate to inform him that the man in question was family to them and whatever they did was out of love for him. She told him Shamsuddin's tragic story and how his family back in the village had plainly denied attending him even at his deathbed.

Shamsuddin heard every word of the conversation. He was overwhelmed to know that his two angels never left his side. In fact their attempt to reunite him with his family left him obliged. He knew well that he could never repay their debt anymore yet he prayed for their welfare. He wanted to thank Latika for all the generosity she had shown towards him. He bowed to her although he knew she cannot see him as he was a mere soul now.

He was very sad to know that his family had refused to attend him at his deathbed. He had never assumed such an act from Amina. How could she forget the good times they had once shared? Also how mean of her to forget that he was the father of her children. And whatever made her stop tracing Adila and her family? He was filled with grief to have loved a stonehearted lady all his life.

Loosing Adila and her family was the last straw in his life. He had no reason to live for anymore. He was thankful to Allah for taking his life. And this time he had no qualms. He wiped his tears and stood quietly beside his body wondering what was coming next. He had heard of afterlife when he was alive.

""Farishte" (Angels) come to take the good souls to"Jannat" (Heaven) while "Shaitan" (Demons) comes to take the bad souls to"Jahannum" (Hell)"

He waited to see who turn in for him.

Dawn was slowly breaking when Snehlata walked in. She saw Shamsuddin's lifeless body. Over all these years he had occupied a special place in her heart. No matter his religion and status he had been like a son to her. He had always been at her side when she needed someone. She was heartbroken to see that no one from his family was beside him in his last minutes. She remembered how miserly he lived to save enough money to make his own house. It had been his only dream in life and how the house itself had been the very cause of his death too. She could not stop her tears from rolling down her cheeks. Shamsuddin stood beside her as she wiped her eyes but like others she too had no clue about it.

****

"He is not unclaimed, *Pishi*. We will do everything for his last journey. What if his family is not here? We are no less than one. I have informed Nayanmoni too. He is on the way with others," informed Latika consoling her aunt.

But Snehlata was hysterical. "Poor soul! He had passed his days in footpath, barn and all sorts of places for survival in this big city. All he ever dreamt was a place of his own. You know he had been saving money with me all these years for it. But see the man is dead within months after shifting to one. Had he still lived with me he would have been alive today." She sobbed bitterly.

A little later she wiped her tears and said, "Well, now that he is gone his Grave shall be his abode in this big city. Nothing can snatch that away from him. He shall live his dream no matter the other way round." Suddenly the thought brighten her up.

"Yes. You are right *Pishi*. At last he will have his own place to rest peacefully," agreed Latika.

Shamsuddin stood beside them listening to their conversation. Strangely, he felt better in a different way with the thought.

"A place of his own in this big city. No matter if it was his own grave."

For a poor man like him, his dead body would have remained unclaimed in the municipality morgue for days or experimented upon by the medical students of some college. He considered himself lucky. His body was not only claimed but his angels were making arrangements for his last journey. He looked at his death as a new beginning now. A smile swept on his lips as he thought about it.

Meanwhile Nayanmoni and Sachin too came and completed the necessary paper work. The local Muslim community was informed about the cremation and they arrived shortly afterwards. They took Shamsuddin's dead body under their possession and performed all the rituals of the last rites in their religious way. Snehlata paid for all the expenses and ensured everything was followed properly for the peace of the departed soul. Finally Shamsuddin's body was taken for cremation in the local graveyard with all due respect.

******

Shamsuddin now lay buried in his grave in the local graveyard. He had never experienced so much peace in his life before. Suddenly all chains of burden were lifted off him. He felt light like a feather. He had nothing to worry, nothing to long for. All his earthly ties had ceased to exist the moment he stepped onto this grave. It was the starting of a new beginning for him. A beginning with no obligation and expectation. There was nothing he yearned for anymore.

The grave was his abode now in this big city where survival itself had always been a question mark for him. He filled with pride even thinking about it. How many people like him owned a grave in this big city? He thanked his Allah once more for sending the two angels in his life that not only cared for him when he was alive but even after his death.

He now lay at peace waiting for the celestial command from his Allah to begin the chapter of the afterlife. Till then this grave would be his home where he would not have to take orders or serve others like he use to when had to share a place to stay. He remembered how he had to do all the cooking, cleaning and washing after a hectic day's work for sharing the room at Jamal's and Geeta's place. The later had been very demanding and abusive and he still had to share it with her as he could not afford to stay on his own.

Snehlata's house had given him lots of love and affection but the barrier of society, the Hindu Muslim stigma, had compelled him to use the barn to rest at night only. Each morning after tea he would move out of the house to avoid any further accusation on the old lady by the community and return only after sun down to sleep. Allowing a Muslim to enter the house premises was a sin itself in the eyes of the Hindu community let alone providing a shelter. And Shamsuddin knew that Snehlata was always looked down upon by her neighbors for showing this favor to him. In his own ways he repaid her debt by doing petty jobs for her. But now he was the master of his grave. No one and nothing can ever take it away from him. He closed his eyes and rested in peace forever.

****

Shamsuddin lay peacefully in his garve. Nevertheless, forever seemed too short for him as he could hear voices now. One of the voices was very clear and very distinct to his ears. Initially he thought he was dreaming but then he was dead. He cannot dream. He was just a soul. Shamsuddin opened his eyes and paid attention to find the source of the sound.

"Get off me!! You son of a bitch! Get off me now!! " The voice was coming from beneath him.

Shamsuddin was startled and got up. What he saw next gave him goose bumps.

Beneath his grave lay another soul. It was the soul of a shabbily dressed old man in lungee and vest. He was in sixties wearing a skull cap and his beard flowed till his chest.

Adjusting his big rimmed glasses he saw Shamsuddin who stood zapped looking at him.

"Get me up. You fool!" shouted the old man putting across his arm to Shamsuddin.

"*Ho Chacha*," saying Shamsuddin helped him get up.

"You thought you are alone here! Look around. There are many like you," snapped the old man.

Shamsuddin looked around. The place was full of souls. Man, women, children of all ages flocked around him. He was not alone anymore. All came to see him.

"What is your name?" asked the old man.

"Shamsuddin, *Chacha*."

"You are surprised to see them?" he asked.

"*Ho Chacha*," replied Shamsuddin nodding his head.

The old man smothered his white beard and turned to him, "Where will these souls go after death? Till the Allah permits they are all here to stay. This is your new community now. And Like everybody else you too have to abide by the laws of the community."

"Rules?? What Rules??" asked Shamsuddin.

"You shall work for me as long as you share my grave," replied the old man.

"Share your grave??" Shamsuddin could not believe what he just heard.

"Yes." The old man pointed to the garve and continued, "The grave where you lay so peacefully is mine. I was the only occupant till they buried you. And hence you have to do as I say till you stay here."

"I……..do not understand," urged Shamsuddin.

"My young friend with the city growing every year in leaps and bounds, there is very little space left for souls like us to rest peacefully. So whenever a grave is two or three years old it is recycled for use. Thus my friend I am sharing my grave with you with or without my pleasure. So, as long as you rest in my grave you provide me with your services. Same as paying rent when you were alive. This is the rule here and everyone adheres to it," explained the old man.

The old man's wording was a bolt from the blue for Shamsuddin. He couldnot believe what he just heard. How can he be reliving the same life even after his death?? He had to provide his services for sharing accommodation!! He started crying bitterly. His world even after his death seemed unchanged. Why is it so hard to find peace even after death in these big cities? He cried for the ill fated day when he decided to come here leaving his family and friends behind in the village. He wished he had thought twice before heading for the big city but then it was already late.

The end